*"Do you let your guard down with anyone?" Chase asked.*

"With friends I can trust," Jillian said honestly.

"And you don't trust me."

"How can I?"

"Because I'm giving you my word that you can."

She shook her head. "That's not nearly enough."

"Then maybe this will be."

Jillian had known seductive kisses. But in Chase's kiss, there were so many elements that she couldn't name them all. There was excitement and need and desire, but there was challenge, too. There was a determination to break down her guard and to convince her to confide in him, to face the reality that her daughter was his and his daughter was hers and they would be connected for a long time.

When she finally tore away from him, she tried to catch her breath, tried to pretend she was composed when she wasn't, tried to pretend that kiss hadn't been the best kiss she'd ever experienced....

Dear Reader,

It's hard to believe that it's *that* time of year again—and what better way to escape the holiday hysteria than with a good book…or six! Our selections begin with Allison Leigh's *The Truth About the Tycoon*, as a man bent on revenge finds his plans have hit a snag—in the form of the beautiful sister of the man he's out to get.

THE PARKS EMPIRE concludes its six-book run with *The Homecoming* by Gina Wilkins, in which Walter Parks's daughter tries to free her mother from the clutches of her unscrupulous father. Too bad the handsome detective working for her dad is hot on her trail! *The M.D.'s Surprise Family* by Marie Ferrarella is another in her popular miniseries THE BACHELORS OF BLAIR MEMORIAL. This time, a lonely woman looking for a doctor to save her little brother finds both a healer of bodies and of hearts in the handsome neurosurgeon who comes highly recommended. In *A Kiss in the Moonlight*, another in Laurie Paige's SEVEN DEVILS miniseries, a woman can't resist her attraction to the man she let get away—because guilt was pulling her in another direction. But now he's back in her sights—soon to be in her clutches? In Karen Rose Smith's *Which Child Is Mine?* a woman is torn between the child she gave birth to and the one she's been raising. And the only way out seems to be to marry the man who fathered her "daughter." Last, a man decides to reclaim everything he's always wanted, in the form of his biological daughters, and their mother, in Sharon De Vita's *Rightfully His*.

Here's hoping every one of your holiday wishes comes true, and we look forward to celebrating the New Year with you.

All the best,

Gail Chasan
Senior Editor

Please address questions and book requests to:
Silhouette Reader Service
U.S.: 3010 Walden Ave., P.O. Box 1325, Buffalo, NY 14269
Canadian: P.O. Box 609, Fort Erie, Ont. L2A 5X3

# Which Child Is Mine?

## KAREN ROSE SMITH

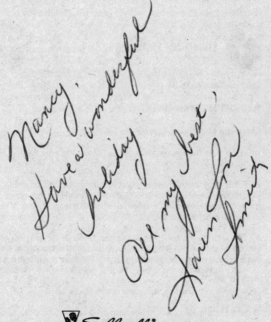

Mancy,
Have a wonderful
holiday.
All my best,
Karen Rose Smith

Silhouette®

# SPECIAL EDITION®

Published by Silhouette Books

**America's Publisher of Contemporary Romance**

I wish to thank Pennsylvania vintners John G. Kramb
of Adams County Winery and John A. Nordberg
of Laurel Mountain Vineyard and Winery who
so patiently answered my research questions.

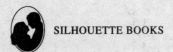 SILHOUETTE BOOKS

ISBN 0-373-24655-2

WHICH CHILD IS MINE?

Copyright © 2004 by Karen Rose Smith

## KAREN ROSE SMITH

grew up in Pennsylvania's Susquehanna Valley and still lives a stone's throw away. She visited several vineyards in the area to develop a setting for *Which Child Is Mine?* She hopes readers enjoy the taste of her home state. They can write to her at P.O. Box 1545, Hanover, PA 17331 or e-mail her through her Web site at www.karenrosesmith.com.

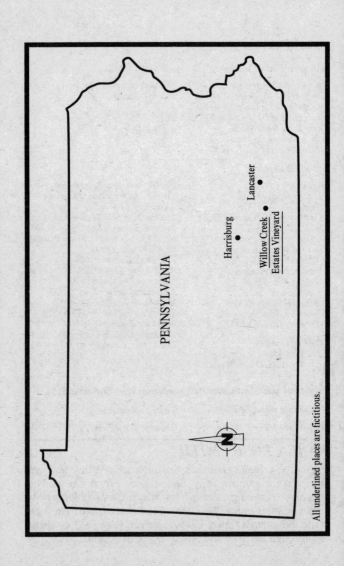

PENNSYLVANIA

Harrisburg

Lancaster

Willow Creek
Estates Vineyard

N

All underlined places are fictitious.

## Prologue

As Chase Remmington held his wife's hand and coached her through another contraction, adrenaline rushed through him, feeding his excitement and concern over Fran. In scrubs with a cap pulled over his brown hair, he was sweating, although the January ice storm was freezing everything in sight outside. Driving to the community hospital not far from Washington, D.C.'s boundaries had been downright dangerous. Although this hospital had been closer to their home and seemed friendly when they'd attended parenting classes, now Chase wished he had taken Fran to a bigger facility. There wasn't enough staff here tonight, and O.B. was overcrowded with women who'd probably come to the hospital in the early stages of labor afraid the weather would keep them homebound later.

The labor and delivery unit was *so* overcrowded, two women in labor lay on beds in the hall. Fran was sharing this room with a younger woman who looked to be in her early twenties. Only one nurse was tending to the two women because of the shortage of help. Before that nurse had closed the curtain between the two beds, Chase had gotten a glimpse of the younger woman. No one was with her. Chase couldn't imagine letting a woman go through this alone. From his vantage point of thirty-five, she seemed too young to be having a baby…too young for the responsibilities a child would bring. He and Fran had wanted their baby, but even *he* was awed by the monumental immensities of parenting.

Fran's obstetrician rushed into the room. Dr. Fenneker was a harried-looking woman tonight, with ash-blond hair straggling from under her scrub cap and tortoiseshell glasses perched high on her nose. As Dr. Fenneker examined Fran, the nurse who had been guiding the other patient through *her* breathing and contractions called from behind the curtain at Chase's back, "This baby's crowning!"

"This one is, too. You're going to have to deliver Mrs. Kendall," Dr. Fenneker returned.

The nurse threw back the curtain between the beds and her voice was shaky. "Are you sure I have to do the delivery? Dr. Singer said he'd be in—"

"Dr. Singer is delivering twins down in two. You can do this. If Fran gives me two good pushes and gets this baby out, I'll help you."

"I have to push!" Mrs. Kendall announced in a strained voice.

Chase heard the fear, but concentrated on Fran's frantic squeeze of his hand. "Easy," he whispered to her.

"The baby's coming," the nurse called.

"So is this one," Dr. Fenneker muttered in a wry tone from the foot of Fran's bed. "Do what you were taught. I'll be over as soon as I can."

Just then Fran let out a piercing cry and pushed with all her might.

Chase could almost feel her pain and just wanted it over.

Seconds later, Dr. Fenneker was easing the baby from Fran's body. "You have a little girl," she announced triumphantly.

Love overwhelmed Chase for both his wife and the child...*his* daughter.

"This one's a girl, too," the nurse at the second bed said shakily, as both women suctioned and cleaned the babies, then clamped the umbilical cords.

Bending toward Fran, Chase murmured everything he was feeling.

After the doctor cut the umbilical cord, she laid their baby on a cart at the foot of both beds beside Mrs. Kendall's new daughter. Then she helped Fran deliver the afterbirth.

Suddenly the lights flickered, and the delivery room as well as the hall went dark.

Gripping his wife's hand, Chase assured her, "It's all right. The lights will be back on in a minute. Certainly there's a backup generator."

There was a shout from the hall. "The generator's not taking over. We're checking it."

Both babies were wailing now, and as the nurse and

doctor moved about the room, Chase heard the cart swivel at the foot of the bed.

A moment later, he noticed Fran's hand growing clammy.

Leaning down to her, he asked, "Fran?"

The nurse switched on a battery-powered light, setting it on the counter. Dr. Fenneker was attending to Mrs. Kendall. There were no lights from monitors now…no reassuring beeps.

In the shadows, Chase tried to find his baby daughter. The nurse was standing at the cart, and he couldn't see the babies. Seconds later she brought their daughter to them and nestled her into Fran's arm.

But Fran didn't say anything. In the eerie shadows, Chase knew something was wrong.

"Doctor? Doctor Fenneker? Check my wife."

The lights flashed on again.

Immediately, Chase spotted how pale Fran had become. Then he saw the tremendous amount of blood on the sheet.

At Chase's call, the doctor rushed over from Mrs. Kendall's bed.

Then chaos reigned.

## Chapter One

Chase Remmington didn't even blink at twists of fate in his life anymore. He'd had enough for three lifetimes. This last one, though, was more life-shattering than any that had gone before.

As he approached the park, his long stride quickened and his suit coat flapped with the breeze. His jacket hadn't been quite adequate for a Pennsylvania winter, but here in Florida it was entirely too warm, even in mid-February.

When his gaze settled on the mother and child in the Daytona Beach park, his attention became riveted on them, and nothing else mattered. Although most of his focus zoomed in on the three-year-old little girl who *could* be his biological daughter, he couldn't help but notice Jillian Kendall, too—the woman who had delivered a baby the same night as Fran had…in the same room. A few moments of confusion and chaos had connected their lives in a way neither of them ever could have imagined.

Chase had never been a master at handling people. Fran had understood and accepted that. More than once she'd told him he was far too blunt, but usually with a smile that said she admired that quality. Now, however, he knew he had to handle Jillian Kendall with kid gloves when all he wanted to do was return to Marianne and make sure her condition hadn't worsened, sit beside her and read her stories that usually made her eyes sparkle.

With another glance at Jillian Kendall, he noticed how her chestnut hair glimmered with red strands in the sunlight, how her face was even more beautiful three years after the birth of her daughter. He'd only had a glimpse of her that night. But he'd remembered her.

Or maybe he saw her face in Marianne's every time the little girl smiled.

Jillian was smiling now. She pushed her daughter in the child's swing. From his private investigator's report he knew she'd named her little girl Abby. Abby. His daughter...

Jillian seemed surprised when Chase approached her, cutting across the grass in a direct path from the sidewalk. But she didn't appear wary, which told him she was either naive or confident enough to handle whatever situation came her way.

After a heart-filling look at Abby—her shoulder-length, wavy, dark-brown hair and bangs, her dark eyes—his gaze collided with Jillian's. "Mrs. Kendall?"

Her green gaze asked a hundred questions as she answered, "Yes, I'm Jillian Kendall."

He knew she was a widow now, and that could make

things simpler. "My name's Chase Remmington, and I'm here on business that concerns you and your daughter."

Though her hands were already on the child swing, she took a step closer to it. "What kind of business?"

First of all, he wanted to assure her he didn't mean her any harm—at least not physically. "I flew in from Pennsylvania this morning. I manage a vineyard there, Willow Creek Estates. When I arrived at your town house, you weren't there and a neighbor told me you often come to the park with your daughter. I needed to find you as quickly as possible."

Her expression more puzzled than anything else now, Jillian asked, "Why?"

The midday sun was beating down on them. Even in February it felt blazing hot. Abby was getting restless in the swing. Brown waves of hair bounced around her face, and the fine bangs blew in the breeze as she looked up at her mom and asked in a little above a whisper that Chase strained to hear, "I'm hungwy. Can we go home now?"

Jillian's attention was instantly on her daughter, and she went around to the front of the swing. "We'll go home right now." Whisking Abby from the seat, she held her in her arms.

The three-year-old poked a finger into her mouth, laid her head against her mom's shoulder and eyed Chase shyly.

Chase desperately wanted to hold her, to get to know her and to find out if she was really his daughter. Yet another part of him didn't want to know at all. He didn't want his bond with Marianne tampered with. But it was going to be. Big time.

Dressed in a blue-flowered knit top and jeans, Jillian's clothes fit her in a way that Chase couldn't help but notice. It had been a long time since he had taken note of what a woman wore.

"Since your daughter's hungry and the sun's hot, maybe we could go back to your place and discuss this." He'd take them to lunch, but he didn't want to spill his news in a public place.

As Jillian settled Abby into the stroller that sat not too far from the swing, her face was hidden by her hair. She straightened then, and her gaze met his squarely. "I'm not letting you near my house until you tell me what business we have to discuss. I've never been to Pennsylvania or heard of Willow Creek Estates."

Chase knew Jillian Kendall was an event planner. She was obviously poised and assertive and everything a young woman was supposed to be these days. Unfortunately, he knew he had to drop his bomb before she'd let him into her life.

"We've met before, Jillian. Not officially. My wife delivered a baby the same night you did. In the same room."

Jillian's green eyes went wide. "In D.C.?"

"Yes. I'm not surprised you don't remember me. You were in labor, and they pulled the curtain between the beds for part of the time. Do you remember what happened afterward? The deliveries so close together? And the blackout?"

"Yes, of course I remember. And then your wife—"

"She hemorrhaged," Chase said bluntly. "They lost her in the operating room."

"I'm so terribly sorry."

He could see that Jillian was.

Abby babbled to a toy dog she held snug in her arms.

Not wanting to dwell on what had happened to Fran, he explained simply, "I think a mistake was made that night. I think our daughters were switched. I believe Abby is my daughter. And my daughter, Marianne, is yours."

Jillian's heart-shaped face went pale. "That can't be! The nurse put a bracelet on Abby."

"I think the nurse put the wrong bracelets on the babies. We need to talk about this someplace private."

Jillian Kendall looked absolutely stricken. He watched denial, then panic and fear play over her face as she realized what he suspected might be true.

Suddenly Abby was jiggling the stroller, kicking her legs and motioning to her mom. "Go home, Mommy. Bow-Wow's hungwy, too."

Jillian placed her hand on her daughter's head. "Okay, Bitsy-bug. We're going home."

For some illogical reason Chase wanted to put his arms around Jillian Kendall. Yet he knew that was crazy. Instead, much more practically, he tried to distance himself a little. "Mrs. Kendall…"

"It's Jillian," she said in a low voice. "Let's go back to my place and I'll fix something for lunch. After I get Abby settled, you can tell me everything you have to tell me. But you'd better have more than a wispy idea about this supposed mistake."

"I do have more," he said brusquely.

With a last look at him, Jillian took the stroller in hand and started to push her daughter home.

Jillian was shaking as she watched Abby run to the kitchen, ready for lunch. This man was crazy. Mistaken.

He had to be wrong about everything that had happened. But he didn't look crazy or mistaken or sound wrong. He looked...

He looked as if he were in command of the whole world. Tall, broad-shouldered with tobacco-brown eyes that were even darker brown than his hair, he definitely looked out of place in her duplex with its flowers, chintz cushions, homey framed prints and porcelain vases. She'd taught Abby what to touch and what not to touch. She'd taught Abby—

Tears came to Jillian's eyes as she headed to the kitchen after Abby. There, she scooped her into her arms, lifting her to the sink to wash her hands. She didn't give a whit if Chase Remmington thought she was an awful hostess. She needed space from him, and she needed to be close to her daughter. She needed time to absorb the possibility that he was bringing her a truth she didn't want to face.

However, Chase Remmington wasn't going to give her time or space. All of a sudden, he was there, in her blue-and-yellow gingham kitchen, pulling out the chair with the booster seat as if he had done it a thousand times before.

After drying Abby's hands, Jillian lifted her daughter to the seat. Abby usually babbled a mile a minute, but when a stranger was present, shyness took over. It usually didn't last for long, though.

"I'm used to doing this," he said with a remnant of a smile.

She knew they had to talk. She knew they had to straighten this out. But every time she looked at him, her heart fluttered faster. Her pulse raced. Heat flooded her cheeks. With an attempt to stay reasonably calm, she told herself the whole situation was playing havoc with her nervous system.

Stepping away from him, she went to the refrigerator and opened it, staring inside. But she didn't see a thing.

"Mommy, mommy. I'm a lot hungwy. Bow-Wow is, too." Bow-Wow sat on the table as ready as she was. "I want chicken and juice."

Jillian tried to swallow the lump in her throat, but couldn't seem to speak around it.

"Jillian?" Chase asked, coming up behind her.

As she blinked hard and fast, he laid a hand on her shoulder and his voice went low. "I know what this is doing to you."

Pulling herself together, she realized, yes, he probably did know, because he was going through it, too. She couldn't face the compassion in his voice…not if she wanted to stay strong for her daughter. For Abby.

"I'll be okay," she finally murmured. "Just give me a minute."

She felt him back away. She heard him cross to her daughter and ask her if Bow-Wow was her best friend.

Abby answered immediately. "Uh-uh. Mommy's my bestest fwiend."

After Chase stepped away, Jillian didn't feel quite as shaky. She grabbed the orange juice, a container of chicken salad and a cucumber. In a matter of minutes she had put together Abby's lunch and had forgotten about theirs.

As Abby ate her little sandwich with the crust trimmed away, Jillian asked Chase, "What can I get for you? We have ham, cheese…"

"I'm not hungry," he said, mirroring her feelings exactly. "You go ahead and get something for yourself."

Now Jillian's eyes met his. "I can't eat."

"Then let me tell you why I'm here and what I'd like to do."

If she sat down and listened, this whole thing would become more real. However, she saw the determination in Chase Remmington's eyes and knew she had no choice. While Abby poked a slice of cucumber into her mouth, Chase waited for Jillian to be seated. Then he sat at the table across from her.

Jillian watched her daughter eat for a moment, then said, "I don't know if we should talk in front of her."

"I'll tell you my part of this, then maybe you can distract her with a coloring book and crayons while we discuss the rest."

He obviously knew three-year-olds, which meant he was a hands-on dad.

"Abby likes to color," Jillian admitted. "Does your daughter?"

"As much as she likes to paste stickers."

Jillian hadn't bought Abby any stickers yet, but often her daughter played with sticky notes.

When Chase shifted in his chair, he glanced at Abby, then back at Jillian. "My wife and I were living in the D.C. area when she got pregnant. I'm a biochemist and Fran was one of my techs when I met her. We'd been married a year, and as we were both thirty-five, we didn't want to wait to have kids."

Subconsciously, Jillian had catalogued Chase in his late thirties. She'd been right. "You said you live in Pennsylvania now?"

"Yes. On a vineyard near Lancaster. I became a bio-chemist because of the winery where I grew up. But after college I only returned for short visits. Until nine months ago. My father died of a sudden heart attack, and I took over managing the vineyard."

"So you and your daughter live on this Willow Creek Estates?"

"Yes. With my mother. She's been a big help with Marianne since—" He stopped for a moment. "That's why I'm here." Arms crossed on the table, he leaned forward now.

His focus was intense. She could see he was that kind of man. Nothing stood in his way. He seemed to know where he was going, and how to get there. So unlike Eric. In that way, at least. But Eric had taught her a man couldn't be trusted. A man could take advantage of any situation for his own benefit. When Eric had died, she'd made a vow to put Abby first...always to live her life whatever way would benefit her daughter the most. Her daughter.

Jillian swallowed hard again.

Looking over at Abby, Jillian could see she'd finished her sandwich and cucumbers and was moving on to the animal crackers on her plate. The only time she was quiet these days was when she was eating. Was Chase Remmington's daughter as bubbly, vivacious and ener-getic as hers?

How could Abby possibly be *his* daughter?

Chase Remmington's deep voice brought her atten-tion back to him. "I know what you're thinking," he said. "When I look at Marianne, I can't imagine she belongs to someone else."

Jillian's gaze collided with his. The force of the impact shook her, and she knew with certainty that whatever happened, from this moment on, her life would never be the same.

"Tell me the rest," she requested.

Leaning away slightly he went on, "Fran had a difficult pregnancy, but she took it in stride. We both wanted a baby. Her morning sickness lasted the whole nine months. But she was a trouper. When she went into labor, we thought we had the world and our whole lives in front of us."

So different from her own labor, Jillian thought. She'd been trying to absorb Eric's betrayal, trying to absorb her decision to forgive him, to go on with their marriage. And it had all been so uncertain.

"Did your wife have a long labor?" Jillian asked gently.

"Terribly long. Twelve hours. She was exhausted by the time they moved her to the delivery suite. You were already there."

Jillian had been fully dilated when they'd moved *her* into the delivery suite. Even so, she'd noticed the women in the hall who weren't as far along with their labor and realized O.B. was overcrowded that night. Then she'd become involved in pushing Abby into the world. That had become her entire focus. After they'd brought Fran Remmington into the room, the nurse had pulled the curtain. Jillian now remembered a quick glance at Chase, remembered the look of absolute adoration on his face for his wife, and she'd wondered how a woman could find that. At that moment she'd never felt more alone. On the night Abby was born, Eric had been out of town again. Even in the throes of labor pain, she'd wondered who he was with and what he was doing—and if she could ever trust him again.

"We delivered minutes apart," she remembered.

"The doctor was coaching the nurse tending to you. Both of the babies were on the cart afterward."

"Then the lights went out," Jillian murmured.

"Yes, the lights went out. I heard the cart get bumped. It was on wheels." He ran a hand through his hair. "My private investigator found the nurse. She admitted that ever since that night she'd been afraid she'd put the wrong bracelets on the babies."

"Why didn't she come forward? Why didn't she say something?"

"She's a single mother. She was then, too. She didn't want to take the chance of losing her job."

"So how did you find out about this? What made you suspect the babies were switched?"

At that moment, Abby kicked her feet and announced, "All done, Mommy. Can I watch Elmo?"

Usually Jillian only let Abby watch TV or a DVD twice a day. She knew some mothers used both of these things as baby-sitters, but she liked interacting with her daughter whenever she could. She loved playing with and holding her and watching her learn, watching her giggle and seeing her eyes light up with surprise at each adventure. While Abby was occupied playing or napping, Jillian made phone calls and worked on lists and preparations for her events. But most days she could spend a good chunk of her time with Abby.

However, right now an Elmo DVD sounded like a good idea.

Out of her seat in an instant, Jillian took a paper towel from the holder, dampened it and wiped Abby's hands and face. "Okay, Bitsy-bug. Elmo it is."

Abby squirmed and babbled as Jillian lifted her from the booster seat. Sometimes she talked so fast it was hard for Jillian to switch into Abby-speak.

After Chase Remmington stood, he pushed his chair in. He seemed to take up all the space in her small kitchen. She could smell a trace scent of woodsy cologne underlaid by pure male, and her stomach somersaulted.

She set Abby on the floor, frustrated by her own reaction to the man. She hadn't dated since Eric died. Dating didn't even make the list of the things she wanted to do in the next five years. So why was she so aware of the potent virility of Chase Remmington?

Five minutes later, Abby was settled on the sofa with three dolls. Bow-Wow sat on her lap, happily engrossed in the Elmo DVD, also. Jillian knew it would keep her daughter's attention for fifteen or twenty minutes.

Crossing to the other side of the room, she took a seat in a chair by the window. A small, cherrywood table separated her from another Queen Anne chair. Chase Remmington sank into it, looking totally out of place. He was too masculine for the chair…too big…too everything.

Concentrating on the reason he was here in her living room, she asked, "So, how did you find out about…the mistake?" *If* there had been a mistake.

"When Fran was rushed to the operating room, Marianne was taken to the nursery. The doctors couldn't save Fran." He paused as if the memories were still vivid for him.

Clearing his throat, he went on. "Afterward, when I

was still trying to absorb what had happened, Marianne's pediatrician came to me and told me he had diagnosed my little girl with ASD—atrial septal defect—a hole in the septum or wall that divides the left and right atrium. He told me most holes close within a year on their own, though if it was still present at two to three years of age, or if she had symptoms, then she'd have to have surgery. Fran's death hit me hard. Thank goodness I had Marianne to concentrate on. I focused on work and her."

After he checked to see if Abby was still engrossed watching the TV, he continued, "A year ago, my dad died. A few months later Marianne and I moved to Willow Creek so I could help my mother. I found a pediatric cardiologist right away. Marianne was doing fine until three weeks ago when a heart murmur developed into a more serious condition. The cardiologist said the right side of her heart is enlarged and surgery is indicated within the next few weeks. I gave blood in case she would need it, and that's when I discovered what happened. There's a discrepancy in our blood types. No one ever noticed it before. She can't be my daughter. After I found that out, I remembered the chaos that night in the delivery room in D.C. The blackout. You delivering at the same time as Fran. I hired a private investigator to track you down."

Jillian's mind raced with all of the information—Marianne's condition, the repercussions that went with it. But then she realized there was another possibility for this whole scenario, one that wouldn't change anything about her life and Abby's.

"I know what you're thinking," Chase said bluntly, reading her mind. "The private investigator suggested immediately that Fran might have had an affair. But she wasn't that type of woman. Nothing in her life or her activities even suggested the possibility. We worked together and spent our free time together. We were hardly ever apart. On the other hand, the nurse admitted she might have made a mistake. That's how we knew which direction to go. There's only one way we'll know for certain—DNA testing."

"Before Marianne's surgery?" Jillian asked.

"No. She might not be able to wait. I went to a judge and requested a temporary guardianship order so I could make decisions about her health in case I couldn't find you."

Fear rushed through Jillian along with uncertainty and confusion. Chase Remmington had legal custody of Marianne. If he was truly Abby's father, he would have claim to both girls.

"Mr. Remmington," she began, needing to put some distance between them.

"It's Chase."

Ignoring that she went on, "You've barged into my life expecting me to believe all of this."

He pulled a sheaf of papers from his inside jacket pocket. "I've barged into your life, but I do have documentation for everything I've told you. I have the cardiologist's report of Marianne's condition. I have a transcript of the P.I.'s conversation with the nurse. I also have my driver's license, social security card and professional affiliation ID if you need to see those, too."

Jillian's cheeks felt hot and she realized he was one step ahead of her all the way. She had to catch up. He had legal claim to Marianne now and if Abby *was* his daughter…

He held out the papers to her and she took them.

Then he stood, towering over her, reaching into his back pocket for his wallet. She was no shrinking violet. She was five foot eight and had never considered herself fragile. But sitting before Chase Remmington she felt much too…feminine…much too overpowered.

She was trying to absorb the words on the first sheet of paper when he held out his driver's license and social security card. Her fingertips brushed his palm when she took them. The electric charge was so cogent her startled gaze lifted to his. His expression was blank, his eyes unreadable. There was no indication he'd felt anything.

That's the way it should be. That's the way it had to be.

Chase didn't seat himself again, just stood there as she read everything.

After she finished the doctor's report, he asked, "Do you have any questions?"

"Is Marianne in danger while she waits for surgery?"

The shuttered expression in Chase's eyes became filled with pain. "The doctor doesn't believe so. That's why the surgery is scheduled for next week instead of tomorrow. But that could change at any moment, and we all know that. My mother's watching over her closely. If there's any indication her condition's worse, she'll call an ambulance and have her rushed to the hospital. I wanted to find you, if I could, before her operation."

"Because there's a chance," Jillian's voice caught, "she might not make it?"

"There's risk attached to any surgery," Chase stated matter-of-factly.

"Thank you for finding me. If she's my daughter…"

"What's your blood type?" he asked.

"AB. Eric's was B."

"And what's Abby's?"

"A."

"Marianne's blood type is AB," Chase said. "Mine is O. Fran was A. So Abby could belong to you and Eric or to me and Fran. But Marianne only matches you."

Jillian murmured, "Unless your wife had an affair with a man who had a B blood type." She lowered the cardiologist's report to her lap. "What do you want me to do? Set up an appointment with Abby's doctor for DNA testing?"

"No. I want you and Abby to return to Pennsylvania with me, today if possible. Just say the word and I'll book our flights."

Jillian had a business to run and obligations that went with it. But she had a partner, too, and Kara could handle everything if she had to. She might have to hire extra help....

If Marianne was her daughter, nothing would keep Jillian from her. She had to fly to Pennsylvania. She had no choice.

"I'm an event planner. I'll have to call my partner and figure out how she'll handle the details of this weekend's parties. But one way or another, Mr. Remmington, we'll work it out." Collecting the papers in her lap, Jillian stood, his driver's license and social security card still in her right hand.

"The name is Chase," he said again. "You're making the right decision."

His voice was low and sure and trembled through her, as intensely as her fear of what would happen next.

She looked down at his driver's license and then up

into his eyes. She had to keep her equilibrium. She'd get through this just as she'd gotten through everything else. "All right…Chase."

Handing him his papers and ID cards, she went to the phone to call Kara, hoping her best friend would give her words of wisdom to hold on to.

## Chapter Two

As Chase lowered himself into the aisle seat of the jet-liner, Jillian sat in the seat next to him, then belted in Abby at the window. The three-year-old had a thousand questions. Her eyes were bright, and her mouth rounded as she looked out the window, intent on all the activity below.

Chase thought about earlier in the afternoon when Jillian had called her partner, made a few other calls, then quickly packed for her and Abby, telling her daughter they were flying to Chase's home to visit his family. She was a single mom with lots of responsibility. She seemed to be a good mother, though he didn't quite understand the ins and outs of her life yet, or how she managed the business and a child without letting either suffer. If he needed it, he did have the name and address of a woman who supposedly cared for Abby when Jillian worked. The P.I. had gotten him a lot of information in a short amount of time.

He and Jillian didn't speak as the other passengers loaded. After the flight attendant went through the emergency procedures, Jillian held Abby's hand and bent her head close to her daughter's while the plane took off.

"Have you flown much?" Chase asked her.

She shook her head. "No. Not much. I took a couple of business trips with my husband before Abby was born. But we drove to Florida when we moved from D.C."

"The three of you?"

Her face became shadowed, and she shook her head. "No. We moved after Eric died."

Maybe he felt a bond with Jillian because they'd both lost a spouse. "Loss is something you never get over." He still felt as if Fran held a piece of his heart.

"Loss, in any form, is hard to handle," Jillian said quietly.

He would have asked her what she meant, but she leaned toward Abby then, lowering the serving tray so the little girl could color.

They'd been flying only a short time it seemed when the flight attendant served beverages and a small snack. Abby chewed the little pretzels. Pictures of Marianne filled Chase's head, and he hoped she didn't miss him too much. He hoped his mother was occupying Marianne with quiet activities. Worry had gnawed at Chase ever since the doctor had told him about Marianne's defect. Maybe finally after she had corrective surgery, that worry would go away.

Offering his bag of open pretzels to Jillian, he asked, "Sure you don't want any?"

Jillian had refused a drink and snack of her own, and although she'd made an omelette for Abby and him earlier, Jillian hadn't eaten then, either. He was tied up in knots, too. Yet he knew for Marianne's sake he had to take care of himself. He wished Jillian would do the same but knew he couldn't force her.

After a brief smile she shook her head and her wavy hair fell enticingly over her shoulders. She was wearing a green cotton blouse and slacks. She'd tucked flannel jackets for her and Abby into the overhead compartment, and he realized now they wouldn't be warm enough in Pennsylvania. But clothing was the least of their problems.

Unable to take his eyes from Jillian, he realized she had a few freckles on her nose. Otherwise, her skin was porcelain perfect. A stir of desire again compromised his need to keep his distance. "You have to eat, Jillian. For Abby's sake, as well as Marianne's."

His words had come out a little sterner than he'd expected. But Jillian didn't retreat…she stood her ground. "I had a huge breakfast this morning. Once we get to Pennsylvania, I'll think about food. Right now I'm better off without it, especially flying."

He supposed the protective feeling that overtook him where Jillian was concerned came from the fact that he was twelve years older. "You must have married young," he commented.

Jillian blinked at the change of subject. "I was twenty-one, although I don't know how young that is."

From the report, he knew Eric had been three years older than she was.

Suddenly, forestalling any further conversation on

the subject, Jillian asked, "Could I see those papers again? The guardianship papers and the transcript. I really didn't look at them thoroughly before."

Extracting them from his jacket pocket, he handed them to her.

This time as she studied them he could see she was doing it carefully. "Even though I'm returning with you, you'll be making all the decisions for Marianne," she concluded.

"I came to find you because you might be her mother," he said in a low voice only she could hear. "We'll discuss whatever happens with Marianne together. But, yes, until we have the DNA testing results, I will make final decisions."

He saw wariness flare in her eyes and wondered why she didn't trust what he'd told her. "Even though Abby might be *my* daughter," he said in the same low voice, "*you* have final decisions on everything that happens to her until we know the truth."

"You act as if the truth is a foregone conclusion."

Maybe Jillian was holding on to the scrap of chance that Fran had been unfaithful to him, but he knew better.

With her attention on the papers once more, he saw the shimmer of tears that came to her eyes as she read the transcript and the nurse's statement. She blinked quickly, trying to stay composed.

Chase laid his hand on her arm.

There was instant awareness that went beyond a stranger's comfort. A tear fell from Jillian's lashes, and Chase badly wanted to wipe it away, feel her skin under his thumb, breathe in more of her sweet scent. But his gut churned with guilt. Somehow, touching Jillian made him feel disloyal to Fran. After she'd died, he'd sworn he'd never go through that kind of pain again. Love hurt too much when it ended. Although he'd taken off his wedding ring when he returned to Willow Creek, he still felt married to Fran. And he didn't believe that would ever change.

He pulled his hand away from Jillian and thought about going home.

Before they landed, the pilot gave a report for the weather in Pennsylvania, and it wasn't good. The temperature hovered near freezing, and rain that was falling could become sleet. Abby had fallen asleep during the latter part of the trip, and as they landed she didn't awaken.

Chase said to Jillian, "Let's let the other passengers disembark. Then I'll carry her."

Jillian looked as if she wanted to protest. He saw her bite her lip, weigh her options concerning luggage, the weather and what might come next. Finally, she said, "Thank you. That's probably a good idea."

Chase didn't know what type of woman Jillian was yet, exactly what kind of mother, but he could see her bond with Abby was strong. Loosening her hold on it would be difficult for her.

Although Abby awakened as they deplaned, she didn't protest against Chase carrying her. He explained, "We're going to visit where *I* live."

That seemed to be enough of an explanation for Abby as she poked her thumb into her mouth and laid her head on his shoulder. Chase's chest tightened as he once again thought about the possibility of Abby being his daughter. Somehow, he'd have to convince Jillian to move to Pennsylvania. Somehow, they were going to have to learn to share their daughters.

During the hour-long drive to Willow Creek Estates the weather turned nasty. Snow fell, mixed with an icy rain and Chase had to concentrate on his driving. But he wasn't concentrating so hard that he didn't notice Jillian's glances to the back where Abby was sleeping in Marianne's car seat.

Jillian wrapped her arms around herself.

"Should I hike up the heat?" he asked.

"No. I'm fine."

"This is quite a change from Florida."

"Yes, it is."

Talk about the weather wasn't going to get them much mileage. He could feel Jillian's tension, see it in the set of her shoulders, the tilt of her head. After a few beats of silence, Chase decided to trod in unchartered territory. "Tell me about Abby's father."

"Why?" Jillian's voice was defensive.

"Because he might have been Marianne's father."

Jillian stared at the windshield wipers swishing away the flurries of snow and the pinging sleet. "He was a financial advisor."

Chase already knew that, along with other basics. "What happened?" Chase asked. Although he knew Eric had died of cancer, he wondered how it all started and how Jillian had handled it.

"He developed pancreatic cancer. He came from a small town in Pennsylvania where there were a lot of powder metal factories and a high incident rate of cancer. But, as the doctors say, that's anecdotal. He died five months after he was diagnosed."

"That's tough."

Jillian didn't answer. She just kept staring out the window, and he wondered what she was seeing—other than the icy rain.

"Were he and Abby close?"

"I don't see what this has to do—"

"I want to know how Abby grew up. What role you and Eric played in her life."

Now there was a fiery passion in Jillian's voice. "I loved Abby with all my heart and soul from the moment she was conceived. She was only six months old when Eric got sick. His role in her life wasn't the usual one."

Still, Chase persisted, "He wasn't with you that night—the night you were in labor."

Jillian was silent just a second too long for Chase to believe her answer when she said, "He traveled a lot. He was out of town on business."

Treading carefully just wasn't in Chase's nature, but he had too much at stake to push Jillian or make an enemy of her. Despite the tension between them, her defensiveness and the entire situation, his body responded to her—or his hormones, or whatever made a man desire a woman. He hadn't felt the electric stirrings, the physical need, the inclination to touch someone else in an intimate way, since Fran had died. That he felt it now with this woman made no sense and complicated the situation even further. However, he'd always prided himself on being in control of his emotions, as well as his actions. He could control lust just like all the rest. The invisible touch of Fran's hand on his shoulder would help him because he wasn't about to forget her or what they'd shared.

"You said you and your wife were married a year before she got pregnant?" Jillian asked, turning the conversation back to him.

"I only had twenty-one months with her, and it wasn't nearly enough."

Though he expected Jillian to dig deeper than that, to his surprise, she didn't. She became uncomfortably silent and he wished he could read her mind.

When they arrived at Willow Creek, Chase sensed Jillian reading the floodlit sign marking entry to the private road. It was difficult to see anything with the darkness, the snow and the sleet. But because he was so familiar with Willow Creek, he knew the shadows and darkness, as well as every square acre of the property.

"How big is Willow Creek?" Jillian asked.

"About fifty acres. The trees along this road are silver maples, planted by my grandfather."

The road wound deeper into the rolling vineyard for half a mile, until they came upon first the winery on the right, then a three-story stone and brick house with a wide front porch. The porch light illuminated the wide white door and the pristine trim.

"It's big," Jillian murmured.

"Yes, it is. So there's plenty of room for you and Abby."

Switching on the interior light, he checked on the little girl in the back seat and saw her eyes were open now. He smiled at her. "Let's go meet my mother. I'm sure she'll have a snack waiting for you if you'd like. Maybe some oatmeal cookies."

Abby's gaze went to her mom's. "Can I have cookies?"

Although Chase could see Jillian was still tense, she forced a smile for her daughter. "Sure you can have a cookie."

"Bow-Wow, too?"

Jillian nodded. "Bow-Wow, too."

Chase had called his mother from the airport and alerted her that they'd landed. Confirming his suspicion that she was probably waiting—worried, anxious and excited as well—his mother opened the front door before they were out of the car. Before he could open his door and get to the back seat to release Abby from her seat belt, Jillian was there unfastening the buckle and taking Abby into her arms. It was obvious there was going to be a push-pull here, that she was claiming Abby, protecting her and giving him the message that nothing would harm her daughter. Would she have those same feelings for Marianne?

He knew better than to offer to take Abby. The look in Jillian's eyes said she wasn't giving her up. Not to anyone.

Pulling Abby's little flannel hood onto her head, Jillian mounted the steps, unmindful of her own hair collecting ice and snow.

She stopped in front of Chase's mother, and there was an awkward silence until Jillian said, "Hello, I'm Jillian Kendall."

The older woman nodded curtly before replying, "I'm Eleanor Remmington."

Chase joined them on the porch, having retrieved the suitcases, and now his mother's eyes went to his. "Come in out of the cold," she said before backing up to let them inside and shutting the door against the February wind and weather.

Chase tried to see the house through Jillian's perspective and realized it probably looked terrifically old-fashioned and out of date to her. A large foyer led to a living room on the left. To the right of the foyer, the wide-stepped oak stairway led to the second floor, and a hall continued straight ahead to the kitchen. The wallpaper in the living room hadn't been changed in over a decade. Off-white with large bouquets of cabbage roses, its formality was evident in gold scrolling on cream paper. It was a long, wide room with two overstuffed chairs and ottomans. A sofa, with a multitude of throw pillows that matched the wallpaper, sat across from the fireplace with a stone hearth and a mahogany mantel. At the other end of the room, two leather recliners and a Boston rocker were grouped around an entertainment center.

Chase knew Jillian would see the kitchen as old-fashioned, too. All of the appliances, except for the microwave, were almost two decades old. But his mother kept the cherrywood cupboards polished to a mirrored sheen, and though the green and beige tiled floor and counter had been recent additions in a superficial makeover, they were as immaculate as everything else in the house.

Chase made introductions as casually as he could. "Mom, you've met Jillian and this is Abby." He looked to his mother.

Eleanor's expression said she wanted to claim Abby as Chase's daughter, but it was too early for that yet. Instead, she held out her hand to Jillian.

Balancing Abby in one arm, Jillian took it. But it was a perfunctory shake for both women.

Eleanor's gaze passed over Abby and Jillian once more. "Those clothes aren't going to be suitable for Pennsylvania in February. I hope you brought something warmer."

When Jillian's shoulders squared, she held Abby a little tighter. "Pennsylvania's quite different from Florida. I brought the warmest clothes we have."

Seeing that battle lines were being drawn, Chase tried to cozy up the atmosphere a little. "I told Abby you might have oatmeal cookies for her as a snack before bedtime."

"Of course, I do," she said, her stern expression softening. She reached out to Abby. "Would you like to come with me to get one?"

Abby eyed the woman in her sixties—her brown-and-gray curly hair, her silver wire-rimmed glasses, her navy sweatshirt and casual slacks. Without answering, she tightened her arms around Jillian's neck and buried her face in Jillian's shoulder.

"She's shy with strangers," Jillian explained, patting her daughter's back, but not encouraging her to go to Eleanor.

Instead of attempting the same move as his mother, Chase crossed to Abby and stooped a little to peek at her from a different direction. "Hey, there. I thought you wanted an oatmeal cookie."

Abby held a death grip on Bow-Wow, but she nodded.

"Okay. Then let's go to the kitchen and find them. I think I know where they are—in a special kitty-cat cookie jar. Would you like to see it?"

Again, Abby nodded, but ventured, "Mommy cawwy me," with a certainty Chase knew he wasn't going to shake.

"Sure, Mommy can carry you. Come on. Follow me."

Eleanor looked disappointed, but as he passed her Chase whispered, "Give her some time." Then he led the way, wondering how Marianne was going to fit into this mix and whether she could bring all of them together.

* * *

Forty-five minutes later Jillian found herself in a bedroom with an enormous mahogany sleigh bed, feeling as if she'd landed in Oz. Today events had transpired so rapidly she couldn't quite seem to get her bearings.

"'Night, Mommy," Abby murmured as she turned on her side, holding Bow-Wow closer.

Jillian's heart hurt as she covered her daughter. Eleanor Remmington had intended for Jillian and Abby to sleep in side-by-side bedrooms. But Jillian had vetoed the idea, telling the older woman she and Abby would sleep together tonight. She didn't want Abby to awaken in a strange place and be scared. To her surprise, Chase had backed her up.

Jillian sank onto the bed next to Abby now, wanting to take her into her arms and never let her go. Her mind was telling her she should get ready for bed, too…that she should tumble into the same sleepy world as Abby and try to get a better perspective on everything in the morning. Yet, her thoughts were whirling and her body felt as if she'd had ten cups of caffeine. She'd had none.

The bedroom door creaked open and Chase stepped inside. "I didn't want to knock and wake her if she'd fallen asleep."

Jillian looked down at Abby rather than at him. "I think she's down for the count. It's been a long day."

He came over to stand beside the bed, and Jillian's heart raced faster. She told herself she was simply reacting to the news he'd brought her…the suddenness of her trip…the strange surroundings. But the small, dim lamp by the side of the bed gave the room an intimate feel.

Suddenly needing to be on her feet rather than having him tower over her, Jillian stood. "Your mother doesn't like me." She'd decided to put the issue on the table right now so they could deal with that, too.

"She doesn't know you," he countered.

"That doesn't seem to matter to her."

Chase raked his hand through his hair, and Jillian saw the lines of fatigue on his forehead and around his eyes. He'd had a long day, too. More than one of them.

"This past year hasn't been easy for her. My dad's death was sudden. And even though my uncle tried to step in to help her run the winery, she'd never had to deal with all the aspects of running the business. She'd helped my dad succeed in her own way—being connected to the community, serving on committees, acting as his hostess. But the process of making wine itself overwhelmed her."

"Many women find themselves in that position when their husbands die."

"Did you?" Chase asked.

"No. But I was already running my own business."

"And my mother knows that. She knows you're a widow and a single mom making it on your own. That could be why she seems defensive. Maybe she sees you as the type of woman she always wanted to be—independent with a career of her own. She's also become protective and proprietary about Marianne. I think our being here has given her life new purpose."

"She sees me as a threat to that?" Jillian asked.

"Possibly."

He was looking down at her pensively, as if he was trying to read or figure out everything about her. As she tried to do the same thing with him, she felt that current between them again like a vibrational field that shook her almost as much as the entire situation.

Finally he asked, "Would you like to see Marianne? She's a sound sleeper. If we go in, you won't wake her."

In a way, Jillian felt as if she'd been holding her breath all afternoon and all evening. Fear had never been a companion to her. She'd always pushed it aside, denied it, stepped around it to do what she had to do. But now she had to face the fear that had been jabbing at her heart ever since Chase Remmington had barged into her life.

What if Abby wasn't her daughter? What if she lost her?

Turning away from Chase, she leaned down to Abby and kissed her cheek. "I'll be right back, Bitsy-bug."

Unwilling to let Chase see her fear, knowing it was a weapon he could use against her, Jillian straightened, calmed herself and said in a quiet voice, "I'd like to see Marianne."

## Chapter Three

As Jillian walked down the silent hall beside Chase, she felt as if she were in a dream. None of today seemed real—not his appearance at the park or the story he'd told her or their flight here. It was almost impossible for her to fathom that, in a few minutes, she might be meeting her own daughter!

A dim light glowed from a room on the right, and when Chase stopped, she did, too.

"She's in here," he said in a low voice.

She could see his love for Marianne as well as pain in his eyes. He was afraid he was going to lose his child to heart surgery or to the condition that surgery was meant to repair.

Standing aside, he let Jillian precede him into the room. She was only minimally aware of the white furniture, the pink-flowered spread and canopy, stuffed animals that probably stood taller than the three-year-old did.

Then she saw the oxygen tank in a corner and stilled.

After a moment, she noticed the dog—a fluffy Pomeranian who nestled on the spread next to Marianne's side.

The dog looked up at Jillian with liquid brown eyes. He hadn't been asleep, but rather guarding his mistress.

Everything inside of Jillian went still as she gazed down at the sleeping child. She had brown hair that was lighter than Abby's. In the glow of the small night lamp she seemed fragile.

Jillian couldn't help but step even closer to the bed and fall onto her knees. Then she saw a baby intercom and a type of monitor on the nightstand.

"The heart monitor is a precaution. If her heart rate changes, an alarm will go off." Chase's voice was a velvet whisper in the darkness.

When Jillian could only stare at Marianne, soaking in everything about her, Chase went on, "I come in two or three times a night to check on her. Even when she wasn't having symptoms, I did that. We have the oxygen tank in case there's an emergency. Hopefully there won't be with surgery scheduled for Monday."

With sudden realization, Jillian saw how hard this had been for him. He didn't show it, and she suspected he didn't talk much about it, either. Not his feelings, anyway. The strong silent type?

She didn't know, and it didn't matter. All that mattered were these two little girls.

The dog was eyeing her warily, and before she reached out to touch Marianne, Chase said, "It's okay, Buff. She won't hurt her."

The little ball of fur seemed to relax at that, and he put his head down on his paws.

"Marianne loves animals," Chase murmured. "She's had Buffington since she was eighteen months old. He's been her companion when I can't be around."

The dog looked older than a pup. "Where did you get him?" she murmured in a low voice.

"A friend. She was moving and couldn't take Buff with her."

Jillian reached toward Marianne and brushed a strand of her chin-length brown hair away from her face. This little girl was precious, too.

Then Jillian stood, overwhelmed with feelings that were all jumbled…sensations that were strange…confusion that didn't seem to have an end. All of their lives were going to change.

Unless Marianne *wasn't* her daughter.

Once more in the hall, she pictured Abby's face in her mind's eye. She'd always thought Abby was a combination of her and Eric. But now— Could that nose have come from Chase's wife? Could her stubborn streak have come from Chase? Were those brown eyes Chase's, not Eric's? Did her genes really belong to a different set of parents?

When she'd gazed at Marianne, Jillian could almost see herself and Eric in her, too, if she looked hard enough…if she imagined.

Jillian was so deep into her emotions, she didn't even realize she was crying until Chase stopped her by putting a hand on her shoulder. "You have to believe it's all going to work out."

"How can it? Unless they weren't switched. Unless…"

"Unless my wife had an affair?" Chase's brow furrowed. "Don't set your hopes on that, Jillian. There's no evidence of it. None whatsoever."

Jillian remembered the transcript she'd read of the P.I.'s conversation with the nurse. "Nurse Holt's memory isn't one hundred percent clear. She isn't sure she put the wrong bracelets on the babies."

"She might not be sure, but she admitted it was a good possibility. And maybe she's still trying to protect herself."

Jillian shook her head. "I can't give up Abby. I *won't* give up Abby. She's *my* daughter."

Moving away from Chase, Jillian felt more alone than she'd ever felt in her life.

Then Chase's arm was around her and he was making her face him. "The girls deserve to know the truth, and we do, too. If you don't face it, it only comes back to bite you."

Suddenly Jillian realized he'd had experience with this—experience with lies…experience with not knowing the truth. She felt as if she'd been through a war. She wanted to get back to Abby. She needed to get some sleep so she could think more clearly. She needed to get perspective for the morning.

However, Chase's words reverberated in her head. Sometimes she thought it would have been better if she'd never known about Eric's affair…if she'd lived in ignorance. Then maybe her heart wouldn't have been broken. Then maybe it wouldn't be so hard for her to trust.

"You look exhausted," Chase noted, gazing down at her as if he really cared how tired she was.

"I just need to crawl in with Abby and get a good night's sleep."

It was totally illogical and didn't belong anywhere in her thoughts right now, but she wondered if Chase had been involved with a woman since his wife had died. He was ruggedly handsome...sexy...confident.

"What are you thinking?" he asked.

"Nothing important." Her cheeks reddened.

"You don't lie well."

"I'm not lying," she returned indignantly, "but you don't have any right to the thoughts in my head."

They stared at each other for a few seconds, the silence as loud as the beating of her heart.

"True," Chase agreed curtly. "I don't have a right to them."

They began walking toward Abby's room again. As they passed the stairway, he commented, "You didn't have supper. Do you want something from the kitchen?"

"No. I'll eat a big breakfast in the morning."

"You have to take care of yourself, Jillian. I don't want another patient on my hands."

"I take care of myself, Mr. Remmington. You don't have to worry about me. I take care of Abby, too. We're only here..." She didn't know how to put it. "We're only here to find out the truth. I want to have the DNA testing done as soon as possible."

"I'll call our family doctor tomorrow."

At the door to Abby's room, she saw Chase glance inside. Circumstances tied them to each other's children, at least for a little while, at least until the DNA results came in. Then their lives would either become simpler or a lot more complicated. It was better now if she kept her distance from Chase Remmington as much as possible. She couldn't let her emotions get the best of her.

She couldn't let the electricity she felt between her and Chase develop into live current.

"She's sleeping." Chase's expression was unreadable.

"She's a sound sleeper. She probably won't wake up until morning. But if she does, I'll be there for her. That's what matters."

After studying her thoroughly, Chase suggested, "Sleep as late as you want."

"Abby's usually up early. I will be, too."

"You don't depend on anyone, do you?"

"No. It's better that way."

Although his brows arched, he didn't ask her why. Finally, he turned and headed for the steps. "I'll see you in the morning."

After he went down the stairs, Jillian entered her bedroom, closed the door and took a nightgown from her suitcase. She quickly undressed, slipped into the gown and then crawled into bed next to her daughter.

Curving her arm around Abby, she tilted her forehead against her daughter's soft, silky hair and prayed for sleep.

Jillian was tying pink ribbons on Abby's pigtails the following morning when there was a knock on her bedroom door.

"Come in," she said automatically, engrossed in forming the tiny bow.

When the door opened, Chase stepped into the room, and her breath caught reflexively. He looked *so* sexy. Instead of a suit, he was wearing jeans and a flannel shirt with the sleeves rolled up his forearms. Although she'd sensed his strength and fitness yesterday, it hadn't been as obvious. His arms were muscled. His thighs encased in the jeans looked powerful. His slim hips and broad shoulders and the shock of dark brown hair over his forehead did funny things to her insides. This Chase Remmington seemed less civilized...more primitive.

"All done?" Abby asked. Jillian knew she hated standing still for even a moment.

With the last tightening of the ribbon, she agreed, "All done."

Chase smiled at the little girl. "How would you like to meet somebody?"

"Who?" Abby asked.

"My little girl. She's your age, and I told her we had visitors."

"Can we?" Abby asked her mother.

"Sure, we can. But Marianne's been sick and she needs to stay quiet, so you can't run around and jump up and down."

"Does she have a cold?" Abby asked, familiar with that because she'd had one a few months before.

"No, this is different than a cold," Chase said. Then honestly, he went on, "It's a problem with her heart."

Crossing to Abby, he crouched down before her. While he held her little hand in his, he placed it on her chest. "Right there. But the doctors are going to fix it soon, and she'll be all better."

"Like me?" Abby asked.

"Just like you," Chase said, with some sadness in his voice. Then he straightened and held his hand out to Abby. "Come on. I'll show you where she is."

To Jillian's astonishment, Abby put her hand in Chase's and went along with him. Apparently, he was no longer a stranger. Apparently, she trusted him enough to follow him.

When they reached Marianne's room, she was lying atop the flowered spread with a white afghan thrown over her. Her Little Mermaid pajamas peeked out from beneath the cover. Propped on three pillows, she smiled at them when they came in.

Chase went over to her, his hand still enclosing Abby's. "Marianne, this is the little friend I told you about. Abby, this is Marianne."

Without even asking, Abby crawled up on top of the bed and sat across from Marianne.

Jillian moved at once. "Maybe you shouldn't do that—"

"It's fine," Chase said. "She gets tired easily and she's in bed most of the time. But she can have company."

Abby glanced shyly at her new friend and picked up one of the stuffed toys on her bed. "Elmo," she said with glee.

Marianne grinned back at her. Obviously, the two girls had found a bond of connection.

Chase said to his daughter, "And this is Jillian, Abby's mother."

Tilting her head, Marianne studied Jillian curiously.

"Hi, honey. We're going to be staying here with your dad and grandmother for a little while."

"When I go to the hospital?" she asked, in such a grown-up fashion that Jillian almost forgot she was three.

"Yes, while you go to the hospital."

"She's been there a few times for tests and doctor's visits."

Abby was examining a tape recorder sitting beside

Marianne's bed. Suddenly as she pushed a button, children's music started playing from it.

Just then, Eleanor came bustling in with a breakfast tray for Marianne, Buffington at her heels. "Oh!" she said in surprise when she came face-to-face with Jillian. To Chase she asked, "Isn't this a lot of commotion for Marianne so early in the morning?"

"She gets tired of being in this room. She gets tired of seeing only us. I think Abby and Jillian will be good for her."

"It's time for breakfast now, though," Eleanor said as she set the tray on an occasional table near the window.

The room was filled with good smells of scrambled eggs and bacon and toast, and Abby looked at her mom. "I'm hungwy, too, Mommy. Can I eat, too?"

"Oh, I don't think so, Bitsy-bug. We'll probably have to go downstairs."

"There's no reason why she can't eat here, too," Chase decided. "There's plenty there for both of them. We just need another glass of milk and juice." He smiled at Abby. "But you have to be careful Buff doesn't snitch your bacon. He likes it too much."

Abby smiled and looked down at the little dog.

Guessing he had another playmate, Buff jumped up on the bed, wiggled his tail, made a circle and plopped down next to Abby.

Eleanor didn't look happy about any of it, and Jillian strove to smooth the waters. "Why don't I go downstairs and get the milk and juice?"

"I'll get it," Eleanor said quickly. "There's more bacon down there, too. I'll bring some of that up."

Chase was already taking the plate over to the girls

and directing Buff to get down off the bed until they'd finished their breakfast.

Marianne looked up at him. "Not hungry, Daddy."

"I know you're not. But I want you to eat just a little bit."

As Jillian stood by the window, Abby ate a piece of bacon with her fingers. Chase coaxed Marianne to drink some milk and then have few bites of egg. With a smile, he made a game of splitting a piece of toast and then handing a half to each girl. As always, Abby ate hers quickly, but Marianne just took tiny nibbles.

Eleanor had disappeared after she'd brought the girls extra bacon and beverages. Now she returned to take the tray.

Jillian noticed that Marianne looked tired and said to Abby, "We'd better go downstairs. Maybe we can explore a little bit."

But Marianne asked, "Can Abby stay and play wif me?"

Unlike Abby, Marianne could pronounce *r* but had trouble with *th*.

Chase looked torn, not knowing what was best for her.

To her surprise, Eleanor said, "I'll stay up here and sit with them for a while if they want to play on the bed. I'll make sure Marianne doesn't get too excited."

"Is that okay with you, Abby?" Chase asked. "I want to take your mom downstairs and get her some breakfast."

After a quick glance at Eleanor, and then a longer look at Marianne, Abby nodded exuberantly. "We can play with Elmo."

Her words came out so fast, Chase chuckled.

"Sounds good to me." He touched Jillian's arm. "Come on. Let's go down to the kitchen. We can come up and check on them in a little while."

Once downstairs, Jillian asked him, "Marianne doesn't have much appetite?"

"Very little. I try to find anything that will tempt her. So does my mother."

Observing that Chase's voice always seemed a bit formal when he talked about his mother, Jillian considered maybe he was brought up that way. "When is surgery on Monday?"

"I'm taking her in around 6:00 a.m."

Once in the kitchen Jillian commented, "I get the feeling your mother doesn't want me to touch anything in here."

"She's worried about Marianne, and she's not used to having company in the house. I think her arthritis bothers her more than she lets on and it makes her grumpy sometimes."

"I think it's more than that. She might want Abby here, but she doesn't want *me* here."

"She doesn't like change. And she definitely doesn't like confusion. All our lives are about both of those right now. But I don't think you'll have any trouble standing your ground with her," he added with a wry smile, coming a step closer.

The top two buttons of Chase's shirt were open and Jillian could see brown chest hair peeking out. Everything about him this morning seemed so overwhelmingly masculine. Because of it, she felt even more off balance and defensive.

"What makes you say that?" she asked, wondering

what he saw when he looked at her…what he saw in what she said and did.

"You're not the type of woman to let anyone step on your toes, push you around or make you do something you don't want to do."

"Are you comparing me to someone?"

After appearing startled for a moment, Chase finally responded, "Maybe I am. Fran took a back seat. Above all else, she believed it was best not to make waves."

"With your mother?"

"Fran and I only stayed at Willow Creek once while we were married. I had business in the area and she wanted to see the winery."

"But it's your home."

"No, it wasn't. I'd made a home in Washington."

"But—"

He cut her off. "I have work to do. But I wanted to make sure you had breakfast before I left. Do you want scrambled eggs and the whole works, or—"

This time she cut *him* off. "Toast and coffee is fine."

Going to the refrigerator, he took out a carton of orange juice and glanced over his shoulder. "I thought you'd promised to have a big breakfast this morning since you didn't eat much yesterday."

"I don't want to take the time now. I want to get back upstairs and make sure Abby isn't tiring out Marianne."

Chase nodded as he set the orange juice on the table. "At nine o'clock, I'll call the doctor and see when we can get the DNA test done. Feel free to explore the grounds with Abby. It'll give her something to do, and Buff loves to run in the vineyard. Don't go too near the creek behind the house, though. It's running full."

He pointed to the coffee in the pot on the counter and the loaf of homemade bread sitting next to it. "Help yourself to anything you want."

Then, taking a leather bomber jacket from a hook, he opened the back door. "Try to make yourself at home, Jillian. I want you and Abby to feel comfortable here."

Before she could blink, he was out the door, and Jillian wondered if he truly wanted her to feel at home, or if he was more interested in Abby feeling at home.

That thought scared her.

Chase waved to Ralph Marlowe as he headed out to the vineyard. Ralph had been working at Willow Creek for thirty years and was in his sixties now. In addition to caring for the horses and gardening, he helped when Chase and his uncle needed him.

As Chase walked between rows of Niagra grapevines, his cell phone rang. After he answered, a familiar male voice asked, "Did you find her?"

Scott Paxton's voice always took Chase back to the football field in high school when he and Scott had been not only teammates but best friends. When Chase had moved back here last year, they'd reconnected as if the intervening twenty years hadn't aged them. Scott had married his high-school sweetheart, Allie, and they'd had two children. One of their kids was in college and the other in high school. After Chase had found out Marianne wasn't his daughter, he'd confided in his friend.

Now he answered his question. "Yes, I found Jillian Kendall...and Abby could be my daughter. I think I see myself in her. I think I see Fran."

"How did she take it?"

"Jillian's still in shock. She wants to believe Fran had an affair and Abby isn't mine."

"I can't say as I blame her. Did she come back with you?"

"Yes. She and Abby are staying at the house."

"How is she acting toward Marianne?"

"My gut twists every time I see her with both girls. She's torn up about this, too. She obviously wants to get close to Marianne if she is her daughter, but she doesn't want to give up any of her bonds with Abby. It's a hell of a mess."

"What's she like, this Jillian Kendall? You said she's a widow."

Chase had told Scott what his private investigator had found out about her. "She's a young widow. She could be a model if she wanted to be. She's only twenty-seven and as independent as all get-out."

"You've noticed a few curves?"

That stopped Chase. Obviously, he had. "They're hard to miss," he conceded.

Scott laughed. "If you're noticing them, that means you're alive. I was beginning to wonder."

"It hasn't been that long—"

"It's been over three years since Fran died. Don't you think it's time you took a look around?"

"Time has nothing to do with it, Scott," he snapped. "If something suddenly happened to Allie, how could you say you'd get serious about another woman in three, four or five years?"

"I didn't say anything about getting serious. I'm talking about getting laid."

Unfortunately, because they'd been friends since high school, Scott thought he could say anything and get away with it. "Enough."

His friend sighed. "So what comes next?"

"DNA testing, and then Marianne's surgery on Monday."

"She's going to be fine."

"That's what I want to believe."

"Do you think this…Jillian…is going to want to be at the hospital with you…watch over Marianne as you will?"

"I don't know her yet."

"You've got a gut instinct."

"I think she'll want to be there. But I think Abby will come first with her until she knows for sure if Marianne is her daughter."

"Could you expect anything different?"

"That's the hell of it. I don't know what to expect on any front. I'm just trying to be prepared for everything and keep Willow Creek succeeding at the same time."

"You could chuck it all and come work for me."

"As what?" Chase asked wryly. Scott owned a sporting goods store and did quite well with it.

"You can manage my store with one arm tied behind you. That's one of the things I always hated about you and liked at the same time. You can do any damned thing you put your mind to—whether it's winning a football game or making superior wines. Speaking of wine-making, how about after Marianne's surgery, you and James and Greg come for dinner? You can bring your best bottles and we'll sample them."

"I'll have to be sure Marianne is okay before I can

leave her. Her activities will be restricted for a couple of weeks…if everything goes well."

"Everything is going to go fine. I'll talk to Allie about planning dinner in a few weeks. Then you can mark your calendar."

"It will be such a relief when Marianne's surgery is over." It would be such a relief when the DNA results were in and they knew the truth. A night with Scott, Greg, James and their wives would be a nice distraction. "Dinner sounds good. I'll give you a call after Marianne's surgery and let you know how it went."

"I've heard Dr. Beckwith is the best."

"He's good with kids, the parents he just tolerates. At least that's what I've heard. Marianne seems to like him, though. And he's been straight with me. That's what matters."

"That's what matters," Scott agreed.

After Chase ended the call, he looked out across the vineyard and let the sight ease his soul.

When Jillian went upstairs after breakfast, she sat with the girls for a little while, talking with them, letting them play quietly while Eleanor went downstairs. Jillian thought Marianne looked too pale this morning. Her thoughts were racing with the idea of DNA testing while Abby chattered to Marianne as if she'd known her all her life. Marianne's quiet responses told Jillian that she was comfortable with Abby, too, and liked her being there.

While the girls got to know each other, Jillian noticed the photograph of Chase and a petite woman with dark brown short-cropped hair. Jillian remembered Fran Remmington even though that memory was dim.

It was midmorning when Eleanor came back to the room, looked at Marianne and said, "I think you'd better rest now, honey."

"We haf to go?" Abby asked Eleanor.

The woman's smile was gentle. "For a while. Why don't you take Buff for a walk? He looks like he needs to stretch his legs." Eleanor glanced at Jillian.

"Is it all right if we walk through the vineyard?"

"I suppose. There's not much to see at this time of year."

Jillian almost smiled at Eleanor's gruffness. It was as if there was a kind woman in there, but she just wasn't sure how to turn her on.

"Everything will be new to us."

"The snow and ice have melted with the sun, so it's going to be muddy."

"We'll watch where we're walking."

"Abby had better wear one of Marianne's coats. It's still cold out there. If you'd like one of my coats…"

"I'll be fine," Jillian assured her. "We won't stay out long."

Ten minutes later, Jillian had bundled Abby in one of Marianne's down coats. It was red with a hood, and white fur framed her face. Watching Abby run after Buffington as he zoomed across the lane away from the barn, Jillian noticed a brick building to the side of the barn and wondered if it was as old as the house and the winery.

Abby continued to run toward rows of posts and vines. The posts were four-foot stakes about eight feet apart. Two wires ran along the top of each trellis. Jillian saw a few orange flags on poles and wondered about their purpose.

She'd only taken a few more steps into the rows of vines when she realized where Buff was headed. Chase was crouched between two rows, one hand on a grapevine as he studied it. Although she didn't want to get caught in another net of conversation with him, especially if it turned personal, she couldn't just ignore him and walk away, either. Besides, she was curious about the vineyard.

Abby and Buff had stopped near one of the poles of orange flags and were peering down into a hole.

Although Chase looked up at Jillian, he didn't get to his feet. "The flags point out groundhog holes."

"Should I tell Abby to stay away from them?"

"No. There's no need for that. We need to flag them so the tractor doesn't drop in."

Chase did rise to his feet then, towering a good six inches above her, and Jillian took a deep lungful of crisp February air. Her jacket wasn't warm enough and she rubbed her arms.

"Cold?" he asked.

"I'm fine." At least she was fine unless she got within two feet of him. Then her heart skipped and ran and her cheeks felt hot. It was a kind of phenomenon she'd never experienced before, and she didn't welcome it now.

His brows drew together at her response as if he didn't believe her for one moment. Unzipping his leather jacket, he shrugged it off. Before she could guess what he was going to do, he'd hung it around her shoulders. It was warm, and she could smell the slight scent of cologne and something masculine underlying it that made warmth spread through her whole body.

When she tried to shrug the coat off and protested, "You need it," he firmly anchored it around her, holding the two lapels. "No. I'm fine like this. I'm used to winter in Pennsylvania. You're not."

She noticed he'd added an insulated vest under the jacket. He was still holding the lapels. His hands were large, scarred and calloused—the hands of a man who worked the land, not the hands of a biochemist.

"Do you know anything about wine?" he asked suddenly.

"I know about types and a little about which years are best because of choosing wines for the parties I plan. But that's about it."

"That's a lot," he decided with a smile. "Most people don't know that."

"What kind of grapes do you grow?"

When he pointed to a small sign, he released the jacket lapels, giving her a chance to breathe normally. "These are Niagara vines."

"White wine, right?"

He looked pleased. "Yes. Catawba are over there. We also grow Aurora, Concord and a few others. I know everything looks dead now, but it's not. The vines will begin flowering in June."

"You said your grandfather owned this vineyard?"

Chase looked out over the acreage with pride and something else—something deep that made her certain he appreciated the land and what it gave them.

"Actually, my great-grandfather started it with about two acres, just as a sideline. Over the years we grew. The whole process depends on the soil and the weather, and we've been fortunate with both."

Reaching out, he touched the nubs on a vine.

"Did you always help your father with the wine?"

Chase's expression grew closed. "Why would you assume that?"

"You grew up here. You know a lot about it. You came back to run the vineyard. You're a biochemist, so I figured that played into it somehow—into the making of the wine."

"That was my original intent when I applied for a biochemistry major. But then— Circumstances took me in a different direction. My father ran the vineyard until he died a year ago."

She had the feeling there was a lot more to the story than that. There were gaps and things that didn't make sense. If Chase loved the land as he seemed to, if he enjoyed the process of wine-making, why hadn't he helped? Why hadn't he come back before now?

Jillian heard Abby giggle, and she turned to see what she was doing. When she did, the leather jacket slipped from her shoulder.

Chase caught it, and once again they were much too close, gazing into each other's eyes. "She's fine," he said. "She found a stone she particularly likes."

"She has a collection," Jillian murmured, looking at her daughter, but much too aware of Chase.

"Marianne isn't a nature buff. I suppose it's because she spent most of her life inside. The city isn't conducive to field wandering, catching leaves in the wind or plucking flowers from a garden. I bought her a pony after we arrived here to lure her outside."

Jillian had seen the barn, but didn't know if it was actually being used.

"She's afraid of him," Chase explained with a shake of his head. "I can't get her on him. And now—"

She knew what he was thinking. That he could lose her. That she'd never ride that pony. "We have to believe that everything will go perfectly. That she'll be happy and well after the surgery."

"You know that old adage, hope for the best but expect the worst? It's become my motto."

"I think the way it goes is—hope for the best but *prepare* for the worst. But I'm not going to think about the worst."

"You're one of those people who create your own reality?"

It was a scoffing question, but she answered it seriously. "I guess I try. Now, anyway. I had hard lessons to learn first."

He was studying her intently, with a light in his eyes that was deep and dark and hungry. "Care to share them?"

Caution bells went off. One of those lessons had been not to give freely…to protect herself from being taken advantage of. "We don't know each other, Chase. We're virtual strangers."

Still very close to her, his breath was white vapor when he spoke. "Strangers, maybe. But we're connected by our girls."

How could a barren vineyard in the middle of a cold February day seem intimate? Yet, standing here with him like this, all she could do was look at his lips. Unbidden, vivid pictures began playing in her head… A scene of him leaning toward her, kissing her—

His large hand was still on the jacket, and now she backed away from him. "We *might* be connected by the girls. We don't know that yet. Did you make an appointment with the doctor?"

"This afternoon at three."

A shout from the house interrupted their conversation. It was Eleanor and she was running toward them. "Chase! It's Marianne! She's having trouble breathing!"

He took off at a dead run. "Call 911. I'll put the oxygen on her."

Jillian rushed to Abby and took her hand, then quickly encouraged her and Buff to run toward the house.

As she felt the warmth of Abby's little hand nestled in hers, as they hurried across the lane, Buff at their heels, her heart hammered and her own chest tightened. If Marianne *was* her daughter—

Holding all thoughts at bay, she lifted Abby into her arms, then rushed up the porch steps. She followed Chase inside, hoping there was something she could do to help, praying she wouldn't lose Marianne...*or* Abby.

## Chapter Four

As the ambulance attendants wheeled the gurney from Marianne's room, Abby stood outside in the hallway looking scared.

Jillian crouched down to her. "They're taking Marianne to the hospital to make her better."

Chase was suddenly at Jillian's elbow, holding it, pulling her up. "Do you want to come along? I'm going to ride in the ambulance."

"Yes, I want to come, but—"

Suddenly Eleanor was bending down to Abby, her arm around the little girl. "How would you like to make sugar cookies with me? And afterward, Buffington and I will take you to see Marianne's pony. What do you think?"

"I wanna see the pony," Abby said with a grin and an exuberant nod of her head.

Still feeling torn, Jillian wasn't sure what to do. Would Abby be all right with Eleanor? Or would she get scared and want her mommy?

Eleanor made a shooing motion with both hands to Jillian and Chase. "We'll be fine. We'll find lots to do. I'm sure Abby would like to play ball with Buffington, too. Go on, now."

Jillian gave her daughter a hug. "I'll call you and see how much fun you're having. Okay?"

Again Abby nodded, lifted her hand and waved. "Bye, Mommy."

If the situation weren't so serious, Jillian would have smiled. Abby was used to her comings and goings. She spent time with Mrs. Carmichael and Kara, too, now and then. Besides that, Jillian took her to a playgroup. Separation anxiety didn't seem to be a worry for Abby.

Thankful for that, Jillian turned to Chase and hurried with him down the stairs.

At first the attendants were reluctant to let Jillian join Chase, but he explained the situation tersely and their reluctance turned to acquiescence.

When Jillian was in the ambulance with him, sitting beside him with their arms brushing, she looked down at Marianne and murmured, "Thank you."

Chase shook his head. "You need to be with her the same as I do."

He was so sure she was Marianne's mother.

As Jillian gazed at the little girl now who was hooked up to an IV and heart monitor with an oxygen cup over her nose and mouth, a blood pressure cuff on her arm, she felt as if she were being ripped in two. She could see herself in Marianne's eyes. If she looked hard enough, she could see the same slant of Eric's jaw on this little girl. Couldn't she?

She lay her hand on Marianne's head. "You're going to be all right. Soon you'll be playing with Abby and racing after Buff across the yard."

Before their flight to Pennsylvania, Chase had explained everything about atrial septal defect. If the surgeon was skilled and everything went as anticipated, they could expect Marianne to make a full recovery in a matter of weeks. But as Jillian had learned a long time ago, life didn't always go as planned.

Thinking about Abby, Jillian worried whether or not to believe she'd be occupied and happy with Eleanor.

Uncannily, Chase read her mind. "My mother's good with children. She'll keep Abby busy so she doesn't miss us...miss you," he amended quickly.

"You already think of yourself as her father, don't you?"

"You're still in shock, Jillian. It's been less than twenty-four hours since I dropped this bomb on you. I've been dealing with it a bit longer. My gut's telling me what I should believe. I have to go with that."

Jillian knew instincts were powerful. Where Abby was concerned and even in business matters, she trusted hers. But when it came to men, she wasn't so sure she could trust her instincts or her judgment.

As a little girl, Jillian had loved her dad desperately. When he'd carried her on his shoulders, she'd felt as if she were on top of the world. He'd been a pro at hide-and-seek. He'd taken her on wagon rides through the park and pushed her on the merry-go-round. But by age six, she'd known he wasn't around a lot, and he didn't come home when he said he would. When she was eight, her father divorced her mother. He often planned visits with Jillian but many times didn't show up. By the time she was ten, she knew her father didn't know the definition of the word *promise* and she'd learned *not* to count on him.

Over the years, Jillian had seen her mother become stronger, more independent, as she learned to stand on her own two feet. That's the type of woman Jillian had known she wanted to become. From a rural town in Vermont, Jillian had decided she wanted a future in a big city. She was just finishing up her business management degree at Columbia when she'd met Eric. He was charming, handsome, had eyes only for her and she fell hard. After a whirlwind courtship, they'd married and moved to Washington, D.C. But after only a year, when Jillian was pregnant, she'd discovered Eric had had an affair. Even then she hadn't wanted to give up for the sake of their child. Eric swore renewed fidelity, but trust had been broken and she couldn't seem to mend it. He still took out-of-town trips and didn't always explain his whereabouts. However, when Abby was born, their daughter took all of Jillian's time and attention until Eric was diagnosed with cancer. She couldn't leave him then, and she'd recommitted herself to him. What kind of woman would she have been if she'd walked out?

So she'd stayed and somehow had taken care of him and Abby, too.

But her experiences, first with her father and then with Eric, had made her self-reliant. She didn't depend on anyone, didn't put her trust in any man. She'd been wrong about Eric's character and the man he'd been. She'd even deluded herself into misjudging his commitment and recommitment. So she didn't trust her instincts where men were concerned, and certainly not with Chase Remmington when the very fabric of her life was at stake.

As the siren on the ambulance kept blaring, the vehicle pulled up at the doors to the hospital. She couldn't begin to fathom where the next few days would lead.

At the emergency room, Chase and Jillian kept up with the gurney as Marianne was wheeled inside. A tall, lean, sandy-haired doctor with wire-rimmed glasses and an unsmiling expression was standing in the doorway to one of the examining rooms.

"Doctor Beckwith can be brusque," Chase told Jillian, "but he's the best."

"Wait here," Beckwith said tersely to the two of them. "I'll be back in a few minutes."

"Won't she be scared?" Jillian asked as Beckwith swept inside the room.

"She knows him. He's a lot gentler with kids than he is with adults."

"Does he know…" She hesitated. "Our situation?"

"Yes. I had to give his office guardianship papers and I explained what was going on before I left to find you."

Wrapping her arms around herself, Jillian couldn't prevent tears from coming to her eyes. "If anything happens to Marianne… It must have been so hard for you for the past few years, watching her, hoping the hole would heal. And when you found out it hadn't—" Her voice broke.

"You understand," Chase said as if he were surprised by that.

Although she didn't want to feel anything for Chase,

there was a bond forming between them. They'd both been single parents. They'd both faced hardships, although he didn't know what hers had been, and she wasn't altogether sure about his. Moments like this when they were standing close, feeling the same worry and connection, her world seemed to spin even faster and she could hardly catch her breath.

The doctor came out the door and left it open so Chase was in clear sight of Marianne. "We're taking her to surgery. I'm going to take care of this now. I explained the repair to you last week. We'll be in surgery about three hours. She'll be in recovery for another two. After that, the first twelve hours should tell the tale. The nurse will bring you the papers you need to sign."

The surgeon would have strode off, but Jillian stepped into his path. "Can we see her before you prep her for surgery?"

The doctor shifted his gaze from Jillian to Chase. "We have to get this moving. I don't want to take any time—"

"A minute," Jillian demanded. "I just need to see her for a minute. I might be her mother. I have no intention of letting her go to surgery without kissing her and giving her my love."

The doctor's severe expression seemed to soften a bit. "Take two minutes, but then you'll have to move out of everyone's way. Chase, I'll meet you in the lounge upstairs after the surgery."

And then he was off and Jillian rushed into the hospital room. Going to Marianne, she saw the little girl's eyelids were already drooping. They must have given her a sedative.

Taking her little hand, Jillian squeezed it, leaned close

and kissed her on the cheek. "I love you, honey. When you wake up, your dad and I'll be waiting for you."

Chase was at Jillian's shoulder then and he was leaning close to Marianne, too. "After this is all over, you'll be able to run and play with Buff again. See you soon, baby."

After Chase kissed Marianne, his hand was on the small of Jillian's back as he guided her out of the room.

Once in the hall, she looked at him, saw the moisture in his eyes and felt her lip begin to quiver. Then Chase's arms were around her and she was leaning her head against his chest, hearing the beating of his heart. He didn't say anything and neither did she.

After a few minutes when she felt more composed, she lifted her head. As he gazed down at her, there was a deep fiery light in his eyes. It scared her and excited her, too. However, in a second he'd banked it and, relieved, she felt him lean away.

Embarrassed, she left the circle of his arms and murmured, "Can we wait here until they wheel her to the operating room?"

"I don't know if we can, but we're going to."

She could tell he didn't want to be any farther away from Marianne than she did. Yet, the comforting and intimate moment they'd just shared had left a lingering awkwardness between them. Maybe it would pass while they waited. Maybe they'd find that connection again. Still, Jillian almost dreaded that connection to Chase Remmington.

It was too dangerous to even consider.

Chase carried coffee and sandwiches on his way back to the waiting room outside of the cardiac surgery suite.

He'd called his mother to tell her Marianne was going into surgery, and then Jillian had talked to Abby for a while. He'd spoken to Abby, too, wanting her to get used to him, get used to his presence in her life. Afterward, Jillian had made a call to her partner in Florida, and he suspected Kara Johnson was more friend than business associate. To give Jillian some privacy, he'd decided to get them something to eat. Not that Jillian would eat. He'd already discovered that when she was emotionally in turmoil, she didn't put food into her mouth.

Passing a nurse in the hall, he thought about Jillian's demand to see Marianne before surgery. She had a fire in her that intrigued him…intrigued him too damn much. Because of that, he thought about Fran and what kind of mother *she* would have been. He realized he couldn't quite imagine it. He realized that whenever he was with Jillian, he didn't think about Fran.

That realization unsettled him.

When he reached the lounge, Jillian wasn't there and he was almost grateful. He handled this kind of situation best solo. Fran used to say when he had a problem to solve or a feeling he didn't want to face, he closed himself in his cave like a bear until he came to terms with whatever it was. His den had been his cave. Now the winery was pretty much his cave, except when his uncle Stan was around. Stan's attitude had been terrifically defensive since Chase had returned to Willow Creek. His father's brother had always helped out at the winery as a sideline and a break from the business of selling insurance. When he'd retired a few years ago, according to Chase's mother, he'd helped out at the winery more and more.

Chase hadn't been close to his uncle since he'd found out the truth about his parents when he was eighteen. Then, everything had fallen apart.

Chase set the box with coffee and sandwiches on the table in front of the sofa. Picking up one of the polystyrene cups, he carried it to the window and gazed out over the grounds.

Time slipped backward.

He'd always respected his father.

Preston Remmington had seen the possibilities of wine-making in the Susquehanna Valley before it became an up-and-coming area for the industry. Chase had always been fascinated by the wine-making process and had decided early to earn a degree in biochemistry, intending that Willow Creek Estates wine would eventually earn a stellar reputation. While he was growing up, he'd always sensed a distance between his parents, though he'd never known why it was there. Then he'd discovered exactly why.

He'd needed his birth certificate to get a passport for a trip to Europe. When he found it in the attic, he couldn't believe his eyes. His mother's name was not on that birth certificate. Doreen Edwards's name was. He'd confronted his parents and learned that his father had had an affair nineteen years before. Eleanor had been a friend of his dad's and had always loved him. Apparently Doreen had been beautiful but had aspired to become a famous singer, and she'd wanted to have an abortion. After his father convinced her to have their baby and give it to him, Eleanor had agreed to bring the child up as hers.

Chase's world had fallen apart that day. He hadn't

even known who he really was anymore, and the first thing he had done was search for Doreen Edwards. He'd found her singing in a resort in Atlantic City. They'd soon understood they had no common ground or bonds and after that meeting, they'd never seen each other again.

Chase knew he'd become an angry young man, unforgiving of what his parents had done, mostly because of the lie they'd told him and fostered. After he'd earned his doctorate, he'd decided to do research in his field instead of returning to Willow Creek. When his work became acclaimed, he'd earned more money than he knew what to do with. With his reputation established, he began taking more free time and noticed the research assistant in his lab—Fran Matthews. He'd married her six months later.

"Chase?" Jillian's soft voice asked.

The sound of his name on her lips jolted him back to the present. When he looked at her, he saw everything that was different from Fran. Jillian's hair had red highlights. She was taller. Her energy was so much more vibrant than Fran's.

He stopped himself there. He shouldn't be making comparisons. He didn't need to make comparisons.

Waving to the coffee table, he said, "I brought sandwiches and coffee."

"I'm not—"

"I know—you're not hungry. But you have to eat anyway. And don't tell me you'll eat supper. I've caught on to *that* ruse."

"It's not a ruse."

As he studied her, he realized it wasn't.

"Half a sandwich," he negotiated. "And I won't bug you about eating again."

"Until supper," she complained with a small smile.

Then tearing her gaze from his, she went over to the sofa and sat. "I went to the nurses' desk to find out if there was any word."

"We won't know anything unless—" He stopped. "Until it's over."

He'd been about to say, "Unless something goes wrong," but neither of them needed to dwell on that.

As he sat beside Jillian, he couldn't deny his attraction to her and the guilt he felt about it. Maybe not the attraction itself, but the sparks that he never experienced in exactly that way with Fran. He wondered if those were the sparks that his father had once felt for Doreen Edwards. He'd gotten the impression that Eleanor had always thought his father had never completely forgotten Doreen, had never fallen out of love with her, and that's why their marriage hadn't been the best it could be. Once a man truly loved a woman, maybe he could never forget her.

During the next hour or so, Jillian kept her thoughts to herself and so did he. They both riffled through magazines they weren't really reading. As she settled on the sofa, he moved to an armchair.

When Dr. Beckwith appeared in the doorway, he was still in his scrubs. "The surgery went well. I'm going to keep Marianne in the pediatric cardiac ICU for the next twelve hours. In about ninety minutes you can sit with her."

Chase went to Beckwith and shook his hand. "Thank you."

Jillian crossed over to them. "Yes, thank you very much."

The doctor shook her hand, too. "No thanks necessary. It's what I do." A moment later, he was gone.

"I feel as if I can breathe again," Jillian said with a slight smile.

"I know what you mean."

Jillian's expression turned serious. "What are we going to do, Chase?"

"Relax for a few minutes and clear our heads."

"No, I don't mean now, I mean— I have a life in Florida. You have one here. The girls got along like sisters this morning. If Marianne truly is my daughter…"

Taking Jillian by the shoulders, he shook his head. "Thinking ahead is going to make you crazy. Let's just get Marianne through her recovery, get the DNA testing done, then we'll decide."

She was looking up at him with wide green eyes that made everything in his body tighten. He knew all the thoughts running through her head because they'd run through his—relocation, shared custody, nothing ever the same again. He wanted the emotional merry-go-round to stop for both of them and he suddenly wanted to quell his curiosity, kick the thought of kissing Jillian out of his head, go back to life the way he'd known it before Marianne's symptoms had made surgery necessary.

The scent of Jillian's perfume was light and airy and seductive. Her knit top delineated her breasts, and he knew they'd fill his hands perfectly. Parts south awakened with his desire, and a hungry need he didn't think he'd ever known claimed him.

When he bent his head to kiss Jillian, he knew she wouldn't pull away. He knew the tugs of attraction between them had been affecting her, too. He also knew Jillian was assertive enough and independent enough that she would have backed away long before now if she didn't want any part of this.

As his head lowered slowly, she whispered, "We shouldn't." He wasn't sure he was meant to hear the thought.

"Should or shouldn't has nothing to do with this," he growled.

Then his arms were around Jillian and he was pulling her close. Her breasts pressed against his flannel shirt. The contact was electric, sparking a fire that built higher and faster as his lips settled on hers. The shock and potency of the kiss rushed through him and he took it deeper, pushing his tongue into her mouth, breaching her world and her defenses. He'd never felt such pure animal need. He'd never let that loose with Fran, but then he'd never felt it so fiercely, either.

The sound of a metal tray clanging to the floor in the hall made him aware of his surroundings again with a jolt. What in the hell was he doing?

With a low oath, he broke the kiss and backed away. "You were right. I shouldn't have done that. Everything is complicated enough."

With a flush on her cheeks, Jillian took responsibility for her part in it. "I guess I let it happen because I was looking for a distraction."

Even though he'd thought it, he didn't like her saying it. "I'm going to take a walk to clear my head." Hopefully the cold would cool down his body, too.

"I'm going to call Abby again. I'll tell your mother the good news."

As Jillian went to the phone, he left the lounge, shoving the kiss out of his head, telling himself it had been an experiment. That was all.

An experiment that had blown up in his face. He should have thought about calling his mother, but he was going to let Jillian take care of it. With enough fresh air, he'd forget about the kiss.

Fifteen minutes later, Chase strode down the sidewalk, his hands in his leather jacket pockets as he fingered a piece of paper in the right one. He'd dropped a phone number in there in case he wanted to use it.

They needed to have the DNA testing done soon. His doctor had told him they could have the results in two weeks, maybe before that if they used a private lab. He wanted them sooner. Everything was on hold until they knew for sure that Jillian was Marianne's mother.

A sudden wind gust had a cutting edge to it but Chase didn't care. As he walked toward the hospital, he stepped to the side of the building, took shelter in an alcove and pulled out his cell phone. Marianne was going to be spending time with Jillian and he wanted to find out exactly what kind of mother and woman she was. You couldn't find that out from a P.I.'s report—not unless there were glaring character flaws.

There weren't.

Still, he had the name of the woman who'd cared for Abby when Jillian was working. If he was lucky, she'd be willing to talk. If he was honest, maybe she'd be willing to confide in him.

He punched in Loretta Carmichael's number and waited.

"Hello?" The voice was chipper. From the P.I.'s report he knew Mrs. Carmichael was in her fifties.

"Mrs. Carmichael?"

"Yes, that's me. Are you selling something? I really don't want to buy replacement windows or storm doors or security systems—"

"No, I'm not selling anything, Mrs. Carmichael. My name is Chase Remmington."

"Remmington? Oh…you're the man who took Jillian and Abby back to Pennsylvania."

"She told you then what that's all about?" He hadn't known how close Jillian and this woman were, but Jillian had made a series of calls before they'd left Florida and Loretta Carmichael must have been one of them.

"My lands, she certainly did. I can't believe it. Switched babies. They make movies-of-the-week about that. I can't believe little Abby isn't hers. Why Abby talks like her Mom and leans her head like her Mom—"

Already Chase could tell that Loretta Carmichael was a chatterer, and he could use that to his advantage. "We're still trying to iron out the whole situation," he said in a tone that was meant to be confiding. "I'd like to be honest with you about why I called."

"An honest man. Just like my Hubert, God rest his soul. I'm so glad to hear that."

Chase shot to the reason why he called. "Mrs. Carmichael—"

"Call me Loretta."

"Loretta. I'm in a strange situation. Jillian is going to be spending a lot of time with my daughter…maybe *her* daughter. I need to know what type of person she is, what type of mother she is. Could you fill me in?"

Loretta didn't hesitate for a moment. "She's a wonderful mother. Even when she's working, she calls me every couple of hours and talks to Abby and sees how she's doing. She takes her to the park. She takes her to a playgroup. She's even gone to classes on how to handle the terrible twos and how to prepare Abby for school."

"It must have been difficult for her when her husband was diagnosed with cancer."

"Difficult? *That's* an understatement. It's just a terrible shame what he put her through."

"You mean his illness?"

"Lord, no. From what Jillian told me, while she was pregnant he had an affair! Wasn't the first, either, if you ask me. But Jillian wanted to believe it was. The poor girl was pregnant…believed in marriage…so she forgave him. She wanted two parents for her baby. I guess there was no faulting her for that, but it sounded to me like Eric wasn't the husband and father type. She said she decided to stick with him, though, and try to trust him again. But he still took those business trips and didn't account for his time, especially after Abby was born. Jillian was so busy taking care of a new baby and trying to keep working. She planned parties for someone else then. I think she had her blinders on."

Stopping to take a breath, she quickly continued, "Now I didn't see any of this firsthand, you know, because she was in D.C. But she told me about it."

"Did they separate when Eric got sick?"

"Separate? That would have been the best thing for Jillian and Abby. But, no. She'd recommitted herself to that marriage, and she didn't let him down when he needed her. She took care of him for five months and brought hospice aides in the last couple of weeks. I don't know how she did it."

An additional picture of Jillian was forming in Chase's mind. She'd been stepped on once, and she wouldn't be stepped on again. She'd trusted once and now what had happened to that trust? She'd been loyal and had had her life turned upside down.

"Jillian is going to come back to Florida, isn't she?" Loretta inquired, worried. "She asked me to keep an eye on her town house."

Instead of responding to her question, Chase said, "You've been a big help."

A few moments went by and he wondered if Loretta Carmichael realized how loose her tongue had been. "She doesn't talk about herself much."

He wasn't surprised. Jillian hadn't given him much information at all. "I'm sure Jillian will keep in touch with you and let you know what's happening."

"I hope she does. I care about her and Abby."

So the conversation wouldn't be any more prolonged, Chase repeated, "Thanks again."

After Loretta Carmichael's quiet goodbye, he wondered if she'd tell Jillian he had called or whether she'd keep it under hat because she'd told him so much. It didn't matter. If Jillian found out, he'd explain he was just gathering information.

And if she gathered information about *him?*

So be it. Then he wouldn't have to tell her why he'd been distant from his father in his adult years...why his relationship now with his mother was still strained.

Everything would come out eventually. It always did. Secrets damaged lives. He had firsthand knowledge of that.

## Chapter Five

Over the next few days, Jillian and Chase took turns sitting with Marianne at the hospital. Jillian had gathered up two of the little girl's favorite stuffed animals and a pile of books. Every time she sat with her, she read her one and gloried in the joy lighting Marianne's eyes when she did. Whenever she arrived in Marianne's room, the three-year-old's smile brightened, and she'd want Jillian to sit on the bed with her. During story time, she cuddled near Jillian's heart.

Jillian felt closer to Marianne each moment she spent with her. Her recovery was going well, and she'd soon be home.

When Jillian was back at Willow Creek, she played with Abby, took her on walks through the vineyard with Buff, visited the horses in the barn—Eleanor's mare Giselle, Marianne's pony Prancer and Chase's big brown-and-white Appaloosa Desperado—and generally learned the lay of the land. Chase was never far from her thoughts…nor was his kiss. She never should have let him kiss her because now that was between them.

Now pictures ran through her head that were even more vivid than before.

Now a look, a glance or a touch was much more potent.

On Saturday morning Jillian and Chase were going to take Abby to the doctor's office where they would have a DNA sample collected with a buccal swab. Jillian had tried to prepare Abby for it, telling her she could take Bow-Wow with her.

Now as they came down the stairs, Abby wanted to know, "Can I take Clawa, too?"

Clara was her favorite doll and Jillian wasn't going to deny her the needed comfort.

"Sure, you can. I'll go along to the kitchen and start breakfast while you find her. I think she's on the sofa in the living room. Would you like cereal or scrambled eggs?"

"Ceweal…with banana."

"Cereal with banana it is," Jillian assured her as Abby ran to the living room and she continued along the hall to the kitchen.

A few feet from the doorway, she heard voices and stopped. The male voice was a determined one, and Jillian didn't recognize it.

"You should sell Willow Creek," he said. "Your relationship with Chase is *never* going to be what it once was. Do you think you can really trust him to stay?"

When there was silence, Jillian knew she shouldn't be listening. Making sure her leather soles sounded on the floor, she took a few steps forward and then went into the kitchen.

Eleanor was sitting at the table. A man, around five-ten, with black hair liberally laced with gray and a full beard, leaned against the counter, a mug of coffee in his hand. He wore a red-and-black flannel shirt and overalls.

As Jillian entered the kitchen, he looked her over, his expression curious and maybe a bit wary.

"Good morning," she said brightly to Eleanor and the stranger.

She and Eleanor had seemed to come to a polite understanding. Eleanor had done everything she could to make Abby feel at home and for that Jillian was grateful. For herself, she wished she could break through some of Eleanor's walls. If she could do that and understand the woman, she might understand Chase better. That was essential if he was going to spend time with Abby.

*Was* Chase only living at Willow Creek temporarily? Did he have plans to move on? And move on to where?

"Morning," Eleanor said, checking out Jillian's outfit of sweater and slacks. "You bought new clothes?"

"Yesterday afternoon while Marianne was napping I shopped a bit—sweaters, jeans and coats for Abby and me."

Eleanor waved to the man standing at the counter. "Stan, this is Jillian Kendall. Jillian, Stan Remmington, my brother-in-law."

Jillian crossed to the man and extended her hand. "It's good to meet you."

Stan shook it, nodded and pulled his hand back. "I hear you're having DNA testing today. Then this whole mystery will be solved."

"Maybe," Jillian responded, still hoping beyond hope that Abby was her daughter.

"I hope it is for everyone's sake," Eleanor responded. Standing, she went to the cupboard and pulled a frying pan from beneath it.

But Jillian stopped her. "Abby just wants cereal this morning and that's fine for me, too."

"I'll make hot chocolate to go with it. Abby likes that. Last night you said Marianne might be coming home tomorrow. I think I'll go in to see her this afternoon."

Jillian could easily read how much Eleanor had missed Marianne. "That's a good idea. She's missed you. If you want to sit with her this afternoon, I'll go in this evening. That's if you don't mind putting Abby to bed."

"I don't mind." Eleanor's gaze met hers. "You've done a wonderful job with that little girl. She's more stubborn than Marianne, a bit more rambunctious, jabbers more, but she listens and she has such a sweet heart. She's taken to Buff as if he's hers."

As if Eleanor suddenly realized she was going on and on, she stopped. She was obviously getting attached to Abby.

"She's always wanted a dog. I told her she could have one when she was five," Jillian offered.

"Is that a magic age?" Stan asked with amusement. "Or are you just postponing the inevitable?"

Jillian laughed. "A little of both, I guess. I'm hoping by five she'll be ready to learn some responsibility."

"They're never too young to teach them that," Chase's uncle agreed. "At five, Chase was dogging his dad all around the winery."

"Did Chase spend a lot of time with his dad?" Jillian asked.

After Stan and Eleanor exchanged a look that Jillian couldn't understand, Eleanor responded, "Chase's dad was his idol, and for Preston, the sun rose and set on Chase."

Jillian didn't understand what had happened or what she'd overheard. *Your relationship with Chase is never going to be what it once was.* "Chase said he left when he went to college and he didn't return except for short visits. Why was that?"

With obvious hesitation, Eleanor looked into the tea-cup sitting on the counter then raised her gaze to Jillian's once more. "You'll have to ask Chase about that."

Jillian knew she couldn't…not yet. She didn't know Chase well enough to ask him to share that kind of information. Did she?

On the other hand, that kiss had broken down a lot of barriers. That kiss had brought them closer. Yet neither of them was acknowledging what had happened. That kiss had shaken her to the very fiber of her soul. But she hadn't let Chase see how affected she'd been. She couldn't let him think she was vulnerable to him—not if there might be a battle about the girls…not if there could be a war over who would maintain custody.

When Abby came running into the kitchen after finding her doll, Jillian lifted her into her arms and introduced her to Stan.

He just smiled and said, "We've met already, haven't we, Abby?"

Abby stayed comfortably safe near Jillian's shoulder, nodded and gave the older man a slight smile. Then she turned to her mommy, put her little hands on each side of Jillian's face and said at warp speed, "I wanna have ceweal with bananas."

Jillian laughed and kissed her little girl's hand, savoring this time when she believed that Abby was still her daughter.

In a week or so, all of that could change.

Abby's eyes grew large as Chase lifted her into a cart and pushed it through the electronically opened doors of the toy store.

"Do you really think the cart is necessary?" Jillian asked.

"She might choose a big toy." There was amusement in his tone.

Jillian wasn't sure what she thought about this whole idea. Abby had been frightened, of course, of a doctor taking a swab of the inside of her cheek. Chase had made her a deal. If she did what the doctor asked, they'd go to a toy store afterward and she could pick out any toy she wanted. He hadn't asked Jillian about the idea first and that bothered her more than anything else.

"What's wrong?" he asked as they passed through shelves of Easter wrap, plastic eggs and multicolored baskets. Easter was almost two months away.

She motioned to the toy store. "You didn't ask me if I approved of this."

He kept walking. "I saw her fear and wanted to side-track her. This was the best way to do it."

"Do you promise Marianne toys whenever she has to do anything hard?"

"Not all the time," he returned defensively. "I like to see her eyes light up. I want to give her anything I can."

"If you give her your love, your time and your attention, that's all she needs."

Pushing the cart to a stop, he pinned Jillian with an intense look. "Sometimes it's hard to feel as if I'm giving her enough of all of those when I have to work. Fortunately, with research, I could set my own hours, come home at lunchtime, go to the lab at night after she was in bed. But with Fran gone, I never felt as if I could give her enough time."

Jillian knew the dilemma of trying to be two parents, and it was so obvious from Chase's voice how much he still missed his wife. Another very good reason not to get too close to him.

As they strode up one aisle then down another, Abby talked a mile a minute, pointing to a Little Mermaid doll, a two-foot stuffed parrot and a learning toy one of the girls in her playgroup had shared with her.

"It's a hard decision," Chase agreed with a smile as Abby picked up the Ariel doll again.

"Don't even think it," Jillian warned him sternly.

He feigned innocence. "What?"

"Of buying *more* than one."

"She doesn't have many of her own things at Willow Creek."

"No, but she can share Marianne's toys. Anything we

buy we're just going to have to pack in our suitcase and take along or send separately."

As soon as the words were out of Jillian's mouth, she wished she hadn't said them. Was that what was going to happen? Or would Abby be staying at Willow Creek?

Quickly turning away from Chase, she grabbed a zoo set from the shelf replete with animals, cages and a ringmaster. As she leaned over the cart and Abby babbled about the tiger and made its roaring sound, Chase said in a low voice, "We're going to have to discuss what we're going to do."

Giving Abby the zoo set to examine more closely, Jillian tried to reply calmly. "Not until the test results come back. There's no point in discussing anything before then."

Maybe she was taking a Scarlett O'Hara philosophy toward all this, but that was the road she had to travel right now. Every minute she spent with Marianne was bringing her closer to the little girl. Every minute she spent with Chase brought her a lot closer to him. She couldn't seem to keep her heart closed yet she knew the farther she opened it, the more she'd get hurt.

Abby was still trying to decide which toy she wanted when Chase's cell phone rang. After checking the caller ID, he said, "Business. I have to take it."

Although he stepped a few feet away, Jillian could see the expression on his face as he listened to the caller.

She also heard Chase ask, "How could they be missing? Ten cases? Stan said he sent them on Monday." After another pause, he replied, "I'll look into it. Those bottles can't be replaced. That's the last we had of that year. I'll get back to you by the end of the day."

Abby had set the zoo set aside and was pushing the

button on a toy that lit up and played music when Chase crossed to the cart.

"Problem?" Jillian asked.

"A shipment of wine didn't get where it was supposed to go. A restaurant in Erie has made us the house choice and they've been a good client for about ten years."

"Your uncle took care of it?"

"He said he did."

"I met him this morning."

Chase's brows arched. "What did you think?"

"He didn't have a lot to say. He seemed nice. Were he and your dad close?"

"Yes, they were."

She thought about asking Chase whether his mother was seriously thinking about selling the vineyard, but that wasn't any of her business. His life wasn't any of her business. At least not now…not yet.

Still, she couldn't help but be curious. "Your uncle said he's always helped out at the winery."

"Yes, he has. He knows the ins and outs almost as well as I do."

"He made it sound as if you might not stay at Willow Creek."

"When I returned with Marianne, I didn't know how long we'd stay."

"Do you want to go back to D.C. and do research?"

"That's a possibility, and I have a few others. Once Marianne is well, I'll just see where life takes us." Then he stopped, apparently realizing once more Abby might be his daughter, not Marianne.

Once Marianne was well, hopefully Jillian would have returned to Florida with Abby. However, she knew if Abby was Chase's daughter, he'd lay claim to her. He'd want to spend time with her.

Florida might be too far away.

When Marianne came home from the hospital, Chase was protective of her. Jillian realized that was natural since her activities would be mildly restricted the first few weeks.

Over a week had flown by since they'd had samples taken at the family doctor's office. But every minute that passed, it seemed Jillian was holding her breath until the DNA results came back. She spent a lot of time with Marianne and Abby but avoided Chase when she could. When she couldn't—she tried *not* to react to him. She tried to back away emotionally. She tried to pretend there was no attraction, although any time they were in the same room or inadvertently touched, her physical re-action to him told her differently.

They'd fallen into the ritual of putting the girls to bed at the same time every night. Abby and Buff would climb into Marianne's big canopy bed, then Jillian and Chase would alternate nights reading them stories.

Tonight after Jillian closed a colorful book about butterflies, Marianne asked her, "Can Abby sleep wif me?"

Jillian glanced at Chase, not knowing what he would think about the idea.

"The question is…" he asked solemnly, "…will you *sleep* if we let Abby stay with you?"

Marianne nodded vigorously.

"There's plenty of room," he said to Jillian.

The bed was queen-size and both girls could be comfortable. But Jillian was already worrying about the bonds forming between the two girls. What happened when they were separated?

Seeing her indecision, he recommended, "Let's do it for one night." To the girls he warned, "If I hear you two on the monitor too late, or if you don't stay in bed, then we won't do it again. Okay?"

After Jillian kissed both girls and pulled the covers up to their chins, she murmured, "Sleep well." Then she gave Buff a pat on the head as he settled at the foot of the bed.

She waited for Chase in the hall a few feet from the door. "I don't know if letting them sleep together is a good idea."

"It's one night, Jillian."

"You decided again without consulting me."

"Did you want a summit meeting?"

The tinge of amusement in his voice rankled. "Maybe I did. You're making decisions for both girls…and for me."

His face went somber. "Is that really the problem?"

"Yes. We're living in your house. We're on your turf. Until those DNA results come in, Abby is still my daughter and I'm still her mother. I make decisions for her."

"Is it troubling you that they're acting like sisters?"

She took a step back so they wouldn't be so close…so she wouldn't feel his body heat. "Yes, it's bothering me. They're getting closer every day. What happens when we have to tear them apart?"

"I know you don't want to, but you have to consider shared custody. Along with that, we have to consider whether we should keep the girls together when they're with one of us, or each take one and then switch after six months." His expression was unreadable.

"Is it so cut and dried for you?" Her heart was breaking at the thought of being separated from Abby, by not having her own daughter with her constantly if what Chase suspected was true.

"Cut and dried? Do you think I want to give up either girl for any length of time? Mothers don't have the market cornered on bonds. If you moved to Pennsylvania, everything would be a lot easier," he snapped.

"I have a business in Florida. I have friends there. So does Abby…along with a support system that's all set up. I had to move my life once. I don't relish doing it again."

"Why did you move to Florida?" Chase asked, his eyes penetrating, looking for the truth.

She wasn't about to tell him *all* of the truth. "Kara was there. We'd always talked about going into business together. It seemed to be the perfect time."

"So you were running toward something rather than away from something?"

Without answering, she asked, "What about you? When you moved to Willow Creek, were you running away from something or toward something?"

His silent frown told her he didn't appreciate the question. Finally he admitted, "At first I thought it was my duty. My mother needed my help. Sales were down. She didn't know what to do about the harvest and the whole process. She's not a wine-maker. She also didn't know if she wanted to keep the vineyard or sell it. I told her I'd help her make the decisions."

"You said *at first* that's why you came."

"After I'd been here a few months, I realized I'd been in a rut back in D.C. I'd been trying to keep my life the same as when Fran and I had lived together there. But it wasn't the same anymore because she was gone. Coming here was good for Marianne."

"And for you?"

He looked away…into the past. "I carry Fran's memories wherever I go. Coming back here was something I needed to do to put a few ghosts to rest." Bringing his gaze back to hers, he said, "And now that I answered your questions, let's go back to mine. Were you running away from something in D.C.?"

"The same as you," Jillian answered offhandedly. "My old life didn't fit anymore."

The truth was, she'd not only run from an old life, but also from Eric's betrayal and the sad memories associated with his illness. However, she didn't want to go into all that with Chase. She had a fear of him knowing her too well.

As his gaze lingered on her face, she was never more aware of her attraction to him. He wore a denim shirt tonight and black jeans. As always, the cuffs of his shirt were rolled back. The aura about him of solid confidence and resolute determination could be intimidating if she let it be. But she wouldn't let it be.

Without warning, he reached out and let his thumb trail down her cheek. She trembled, and she didn't want him to see her reaction to him.

"Do you let your guard down with anyone?" he asked.

"With friends I can trust," she said honestly.

"And you don't trust me."

"How can I?"

"Because I'm giving you my word that you can."

She shook her head. "That's not nearly enough."

"Then maybe this will be."

She would have eluded him. She would have stepped away. But the kiss was such a surprise she didn't have time to form a thought, let alone take an action. In his arms, nothing but the kiss existed and she didn't know who she was. She told herself he'd caught her unawares and that's why the taste of his tongue was so seductively intoxicating…that's why she didn't push away… that's why the need inside of her blossomed and filled her whole body with warm, languid heat. Chase embodied virility. He seemed to be an overwhelming force she had to continually fight against in order to stay safe. But his hand on the back of her head, his fingers lacing in her hair did make her feel safe and that was the paradox.

As his mouth moved over hers and his tongue probed deeper, as his male essence surrounded her and practically lifted her to another dimension, the pounding beat of her heart ran away with her. Every pulse point in her body shimmered from the electric exchange happening between them. His lips seemed as hard as his body one moment, but seductively gentle the next.

Jillian had known seductive kisses. Eric had been a master at that. But in Chase's kiss, there were so many elements that she couldn't name them all. There was excitement and need and desire, but there was challenge, too. There was determination to break down her guard and to convince her to confide in him, to face the reality that her daughter was his and his daughter was hers and they would be connected for a long time.

This chemistry between them was too potent for her to handle along with everything else. The chemistry became pleasure and hunger as the kiss went on and she didn't break away. Her breasts tingled as they pressed into his chest. His lower body was erotically exciting against hers. She hadn't been with a man since she and Eric had tried to put their marriage back together. But that hadn't been like this. That had been duty and re-commitment and trying so hard that pleasure had escaped her.

Chase was giving her so much pleasure now.

He was giving her pleasure. He was trying to convince her…of what? That she should give up her daughter? That she shouldn't go back to Florida?

Men were good at getting their own way and she was sure Chase Remmington wasn't an exception.

Tearing away from him, she tried to catch her breath, tried to pretend she was composed when she wasn't, tried to pretend that kiss hadn't been the best kiss she'd ever experienced.

Grabbing for anything she could think of, grabbing just for words that made sense, she blurted, "I don't know if I can trust you. We're not even friends. And if what you say is true, we could be facing each other in court over a custody battle. So this isn't a good idea."

"A custody battle," he repeated in a grim tone. "Is that where you want this to go?"

"No! But if you want one thing and I want another and we can't agree—"

"We're adults. We can put our daughters first."

"I'm not worried about putting our daughters first. I *am* worried about how you plan to manipulate me into doing what you want."

"You're going to *have* to trust me, Jillian, or this will be a hundred times harder than it has to be."

"For you maybe. But I'm going to protect myself and Abby no matter what I have to do."

Then she was walking away from him, trying to keep herself from *running* away from him. Chase Remmington posed too great a danger to ignore—to her heart, to her emotions and to her life.

Once the DNA results were in, she'd know what to do next.

If she was Marianne's mother, the next step would be consulting a lawyer.

## Chapter Six

On Thursday afternoon Chase was stacking bottles of wine in the boxlike slanted shelves behind the tasting bar when the heavy wooden door from the outside opened and a couple in their mid-twenties stepped inside. They studied the rustic building, taking in the interior stone walls, the beamed ceiling, the racks and tables displaying gifts for any wine connoisseur, the glass doors leading to the winery.

After a quick look around, they crossed to the huge mahogany bar and asked Chase, "Are you open for wine tasting?"

His tasting room manager was only on duty on weekends in March. During the busy season, she was there daily. His father had always enjoyed introducing novices to wine. Chase, however, enjoyed the process of wine-making most.

"Sure. Have a seat." He gestured to the wooden stools in front of the bar.

Extending his hand, he introduced himself and soon, he and Sherry and Tom were on a first-name basis.

"Actually," Sherry said, hitching herself up onto the stool, "we didn't just come for wine tasting." She stole a glance at the man next to her who she'd introduced as her fiancé.

"You'd like to take a tour of the winery and the vineyard?" Chase asked.

"Yes, we'd like a tour," Tom responded, taking over. "But for a specific reason. We want to get married in June. But since we've only just decided…" He squeezed his fiancée's hand with a loving look. "We're having problems finding a venue. So we decided to think outside of the box. A friend mentioned Willow Creek to us and we wondered if you ever hold weddings here?"

A wedding at Willow Creek. Chase was almost positive that had never occurred. "No, I don't think we've ever had a wedding here. It would be quite an undertaking since we're not specifically set up for that."

"We'll pay you," Tom hastened to say. "We could probably find someone to coordinate the whole thing. It doesn't have to be elaborate. We'd only be talking about maybe fifty guests."

A coordinator. An event planner. A wedding planner. Did Jillian do weddings?

Jillian. They hadn't cleared the air after his kiss… after her outburst. Except for dealing with the girls, they'd avoided each other the past few days. He didn't regret kissing her. The moment of temptation had been so damn strong. It was because she seemed to have her guard so firmly in place that he'd just wanted to blast through it. He'd just wanted to relieve some of the tension in his own body every time he was around her. He'd just wanted to find out if a second kiss could be as good as the first.

What he'd found out was the second kiss could lead them right into bed.

Maybe a battle in a courtroom was safer turf.

Chase had kissed Jillian in a reckless stab at reaching for something that had been out of his grasp since Fran had died. Yet on the other hand, he didn't want to move forward. He didn't want to leave his marriage behind.

A wedding at Willow Creek.

Possibilities clicked through his head. He picked up the cordless phone at the end of the bar and pressed speed dial for the house.

Jillian herself picked up.

"Can you come over to the tasting room? I'd like to consult with you on something."

There was a long pause. "Concerning the girls?"

"No, concerning the vineyard."

After another pause, she said, "I'll see if your mother can watch the girls for a few minutes. I'll be right over."

When Jillian entered the tasting room ten minutes later, the whole atmosphere of the place changed. She'd bought herself a turquoise fleece jacket that made it easy to spot her when she was taking walks in the vineyard or a ride on his mother's mare. She was wearing navy leggings and he could see the sweater neckline under her jacket was patterned in navy and red. Her hair was loose and looked silky as if she'd just washed and dried it. His body tightened as he remembered the kiss, and he thought about how hot they'd be together. He pictured her in his bed.

Her gaze landed on his for an instant, took in his jeans and heavy green-and-black flannel shirt. Then her eyes skittered away and she crossed to the couple at the bar.

Chase introduced her to them. A few moments later, he said to Tom and Sherry, "Jillian's an event planner. She can tell you what she thinks about having a wedding here at Willow Creek."

"I'm not sure what you have in mind." Her glance at Chase was wary. It was obvious she felt put on the spot and didn't like it. But Chase did value her opinion on this matter and he did have a good reason for asking her.

"An outside wedding in June," Sherry said as if that were a given. "Something simple...about fifty guests. Our friends said your grounds were so beautiful in spring and summer. We saw the creek with the willows hanging over the bank when we drove in. We'd love to use that for pictures."

Jillian's gaze returned to Chase. "You really want my opinion on this?"

"I wouldn't have asked if I didn't."

She seemed to consider her words carefully. "The creek area is too uneven for the wedding, though you could take good photographs by the willows. I think the grounds behind the winery itself would be much better. I noticed two orange blossom bushes there. They might be blooming in June. I don't know what type of flowers are in the area."

"The gardener plants annuals but there's a bed of forget-me-nots around the birdbath, if I remember correctly," Chase explained. "Mother usually takes photographs of all of it every year. I can find some of those if you're serious about this."

"There would be shading by the maples and the old sycamore," Jillian continued, mapping out a plan. "It would be easy to set up an arbor. We could use canopies and line up the chairs under those for the guests."

"Could we see the area?" Sherry asked eagerly.

"Everything's gray, barren and cold right now," Chase insisted.

"Yes, but I'd like to picture it. Please?" the bride-to-be pleaded.

He smiled. "We can take a look."

Sherry turned to Jillian again. "Could you give us an idea of how much it would cost?"

"I'm not familiar with the prices in Pennsylvania…"

Tom and Sherry's encouraging expression stopped her. "But I can make a few calls."

"Terrific. I can't tell you how happy we'd be if we could have it here," Tom said. "We're beginning to think we'd have to have our wedding in our apartment's courtyard."

Outside, Chase listened to Jillian and Sherry talk as they walked. Sherry was asking about the arbor and Jillian was explaining how they were done and the type of flowers she usually ordered for it. She seemed to have information at her fingertips.

Once at the site, her ideas flowed freely and Sherry grabbed on to many of them. After one look at the area, Jillian pointed out where she'd position the arbor and the chairs, as well as the minister.

Chase knew he couldn't give Sherry and Tom a final decision until he spoke with Jillian and his mother.

After they returned to the tasting room, Jillian said to Chase, "I'm going to go back to the girls."

He let her go, knowing they were going to have a discussion later, knowing this wedding could be a solution to one of his problems.

After he'd closed the tasting room for the afternoon—he'd had a party of five that took some time and later a retired couple who were just looking for something to do on a wintry afternoon—he went to the winery, checked on the vats, tested samples, locked up for the evening and returned to the house.

The aroma of food cooking tantalized him—a roast in the oven with garlic seasoning, the scent of cinnamon from apple cobbler on the counter. He found Jillian sitting at the kitchen table with the cordless phone in hand. She was ending her call when he came in.

Shrugging out of his jacket, he hung it on a peg. "Where is everyone?"

"Marianne and Abby were playing with dolls in Marianne's room, but now your mother's reading to them. I just got a call back from one of the florists I contacted. I'm putting some numbers together for you and Sherry and Tom. Are you seriously considering letting them have their wedding here?"

"Is that such a stretch?"

"No. I imagine the vineyard is beautiful in spring and summer. But putting together a wedding is a lot of work. It won't bother you and your mother to have strangers trampling about?"

"It will only be for one day, maybe two. Just the publicity Willow Creek would get from the wedding would be worth it. I'm sure Mother will agree. We'd only charge them a modest fee for having it here."

"Why are you doing this, Chase? Why did you ask for my input?"

"It's what you do."

"Not here."

"Why *not* do it here?"

"That's what I thought. You see this as a means—"

"Jillian, I don't have some evil intent. I didn't plan for that couple to stop by today. They just did. You're an expert at what they want. I assumed you'd be staying for a few weeks until Marianne recovers."

"Or until we get the results from the DNA test."

"Just for the sake of argument, if you are Marianne's mother, what do you intend to do?"

She went silent, then finally answered, "I don't know."

"Commit to staying here for the next six weeks or so. Plan the wedding for the couple."

She toyed with the edge of the list she'd made. "I have to go back to Florida at some point. I have obligations there."

"I know you do. But even if I'm a hundred percent wrong about the DNA testing, stay and plan the wedding. When you go back to Florida, you can always fly back here for the event itself in June. This isn't going to be an extravaganza. It's just a simple wedding."

"Even simple weddings need a lot of planning."

"Can you imagine leaving Marianne right now?"

She looked pained at that, and he knew he'd hit a raw nerve. "No, I can't."

Instead of using further persuasion, he remained silent.

As she glanced at the phone, she decided, "I need to talk to my partner."

"Talk to her. Then let me know what you decide. I'm going upstairs to relieve Mother."

He knew if he said anything more, Jillian might shut down the whole idea out of sheer defiance. So he didn't say another word but left the kitchen to her, hoping she'd make the best decision for all of them.

After the girls went to bed, Chase was restless and went out to the winery. He had work to do in the office in back of the tasting room and at this time of day he wouldn't be interrupted. Jillian had been distracted at dinner, and he supposed she was thinking about planning a wedding, staying on and what that entailed. Apparently she hadn't been able to reach her partner, but she said she'd keep trying. As he'd suspected, his mother had taken to the idea of a wedding at Willow Creek and, even more, to the possibility of having Abby under their roof for another six weeks.

When Chase unlocked the side door to the storage area in the winery, he saw a light was glowing. Maybe he'd forgotten to switch it off. He took a turn around the vats, then headed for the wine-tasting room and the office beyond. To his surprise, a dim light shone over the computer desk.

When he stepped into the office, he saw Stan hunched over a file folder.

"You're here late," Chase remarked. "I didn't see your truck."

"It's around back," his uncle said gruffly.

Ever since Chase had arrived, Stan had been curt and remote. If it was because of all the years Chase had been out of contact, he wished his uncle would say so.

"Are you checking on that order that was sent to the wrong address?" Chase asked.

"That address was good."

"That address doesn't even exist," Chase said, studying his uncle carefully. "At least that's what the shipping agent told me. In fact, I couldn't find it anywhere in the Rolodex or on the computer. Where do you think you got it?"

"I'm getting older, boy. My memory's not what it used to be. Maybe I just plucked it out of my head."

Something about the way his uncle responded bothered Chase because he hadn't seen any indication Stan's memory was failing.

"Mistakes with shipping can cost us clients. Orders can't always be replicated."

"I've been around this business longer than you have," Stan snapped.

"Then you understand why I'm concerned."

"You have more important concerns than a shipment of wine."

His uncle's voice held a tense undertone. "You mean Marianne?"

"Yes, and Abby…and that woman who's staying here. If Abby's your daughter, is she going to live here?"

"I don't know what will happen. We do have the carriage house if Jillian wants to move here."

Stan snorted. "The carriage house hasn't been used in twenty years. It's not fit for anyone to move into."

"It could be made fit. We could take the old furniture to auction and make a few renovations. It would be perfect for Jillian and Abby."

"All this is more work for Eleanor. She's getting too old to cook and clean for other folk."

"I'm sure she wouldn't have to cook and clean for Jillian. In fact, Jillian would like to be helping out more now at the house but Mother won't let her."

"She wants her out of there."

Silence beat between them until Chase asked, "Mother told you that?"

"Not in so many words. But I can tell. Two grown women in a house is bound to bring trouble."

In the echo of the stone building, Chase heard a soft voice calling his name.

Stepping into the doorway of the office, he saw Jillian coming through the glass doors from the main room of the winery into the tasting room.

"In here," he called. He'd only unlocked the one outside door. Suddenly he wondered why Stan had come in and locked the door behind him. Extra security precautions?

Shoving the folder he'd been perusing into one of the file drawers, Stan exited the office before Jillian came in. After a nod at Jillian, he left the winery without saying good-night to Chase.

As Jillian entered the office, she took Chase's breath away. The cream cashmere sweater she wore was tucked into forest green corduroy slacks. She'd caught her hair back in a ponytail and her heart-shaped face was cameo perfect. She wore no lipstick but her lips were a pretty pink.

"You didn't come over here like that, did you? It's cold out."

"I'm not used to running around in a coat anymore. I notice *you're* not wearing one."

"Okay, I guess that was a bit chauvinistic," he said with a smile.

"A bit," she agreed.

He laughed. It felt good to laugh. He was still worried about Marianne, but it felt good not to be constantly stressed about her condition, too. She seemed to be recovering beautifully.

"I hope I didn't interrupt anything."

"No, you didn't. I'm sorry he's not as friendly as he could be. He took over the winery for a few months, and I'm not sure he's glad my mother called me to come back."

"Maybe it hurt his pride."

"Maybe. But the vineyard was losing money and Stan couldn't turn that around."

"And you could?"

"I made some changes in promotion and added a new retail outlet. The rest will depend on the harvest this year and how successful I am with my wine-making."

There were questions in Jillian's eyes and he wished she'd ask them, but she didn't. She also didn't come any closer to him. He'd noticed that earlier when they were reading to the girls. Whenever she could, Jillian was keeping a good five feet between them. He supposed that was wise.

"Kara returned my call," she said. "She'd forgotten her phone in the car during a reception she'd planned. Anyway, she said she could hold down the fort in Florida except for one event. I'll have to return to Daytona after Easter. I've been helping Senator Grayson plan his daughter's twenty-first birthday party for the past year. I personally handled all the details."

"That shouldn't be a problem. You can just leave Abby here. She's comfortable with us now."

"Or...I can take her along and her baby-sitter can take care of her."

"Does that make any sense, Jillian?"

"I need to think about it, Chase. I'm sure Abby misses home, too."

"Home isn't a place," he said pensively.

"I know that, but that's the point. Abby's home is with me, wherever I go, at least for now."

He didn't want to argue with her or speculate about that again. "Marianne has a checkup with Dr. Beckwith next week. Do you want to come along?"

"Of course I do."

He gave her a steady look. "Don't forget, I have that same concern about Abby."

"How could I possibly forget?" Jillian asked, and although she was still five feet away, he could feel the inexorable pull toward her.

Calling upon memories of his marriage, of Fran's smiling face, he turned to his desk. "I'll be here a few hours. I have book work to do. But I'll stop in and kiss the girls good-night."

Jillian took his words as her cue to leave.

As he watched her retreating back, the sway of her ponytail, he told himself once more his love for Fran would last forever. He couldn't just forget her and move on.

He didn't know if he could ever move on.

* * *

Jillian was helping Marianne paste popcorn puffs on a picture of a lamb she'd drawn the next afternoon when Eleanor came rushing into the living room. "Chase is on the phone with Dr. Liebermann. He said if you want to hear what he has to say—"

When Jillian rose to her feet, she didn't know whether to run to the phone, or hold back the truth for as long as she could. It was like Chase to think of setting up a conference call. He wanted her to hear the verdict directly from the physician so she'd have no doubts.

Did *he* already know the verdict?

"Marianne needs help with the glue bottle," she explained to Eleanor, reluctant to take the call.

"I'll take care of the girls," Eleanor assured her.

After Jillian took the cordless phone from Eleanor's hand, she went to the kitchen for privacy, her heart pounding as she said to Chase, "I'm here."

"Jillian, this is Dr. Liebermann. My receptionist is faxing the report from the lab to Chase as we speak."

Chase was silent but she knew he was there…waiting.

Somehow she found the words that could change their lives. "Go ahead."

"With both your sample and Chase's, I can tell you with ninety-nine point nine percent certainty, Chase is Abby's father and you are Marianne's mother."

She knew the report's determination wasn't as much a blow to Chase as it was to her. This is what he'd believed all along. It confirmed with certainty that his wife hadn't had an affair. To Jillian, however, the world had just toppled over and she sank into a kitchen chair.

"Jillian, are you all right?" Chase's deep voice was worried.

"No, I'm not all right. Nothing's all right."

"I'll be up to the house."

"No. Give me some time. I just need to absorb this. I just need to figure out what to do next."

Clicking off the phone, she set it on the table and stared at it. Modern technology. Science in the new millennium. Progress was supposed to make everything better.

She heard Abby's laughter come floating out from the living room and tears came to her eyes. She blinked hard and fast but nothing could stop them from rolling down her cheeks. Abby, darling Abby. Her little girl. She'd *always* be her little girl.

The kitchen door suddenly flew open and Chase was standing there. "I know," he said simply.

A sob caught in Jillian's throat as pain threatened to tear her heart apart. Yes, he did know. He absolutely did know. She wasn't sure if she moved or he did, but moments later, he had pulled her up into his arms and was holding her tight. As she cried, his hand passed up and down her back in a soothing motion and comfort.

"I know," he said again, not attempting to tell her that everything was going to be all right. Because it wasn't. She'd just lost a child. She was no longer Abby's mother. Just like that. Because of words on a report. Because of a doctor's determination in a blink of an eye.

"You can't try to figure this out now, Jillian. Go easy with yourself."

She wasn't hearing the words that she wanted to hear…words like "Abby's still your daughter. I would never take her away from you." Then she realized Chase couldn't say the words because she couldn't say them to him about Marianne.

What *were* they going to do?

The first thing she was going to do was pull herself together. She couldn't depend on anyone to pull her through this because she had to protect herself and the girls. She didn't know Chase's mind, let alone his heart. They could be adversaries rather than two adults looking in the same direction.

Backing out of his embrace, she stepped away and swept the tears from her cheeks. She couldn't be weak, and she couldn't let him see her vulnerable. Eric had played on all her vulnerabilities including what she thought were her strengths—honesty, loyalty, the ability to commit. He had turned them around on her until their marriage was a sham…until all she'd felt at the end was duty and pity.

"I need time to think about this," she said again. "We can't just start making decisions until we're sure they're the right ones."

"Maybe so, but there's one decision you might have to make sooner rather than later. You need to move to Pennsylvania, Jillian. There's just no way to get around that."

"If your mother is thinking about selling Willow Creek, *you* could move to Florida."

"She hasn't decided whether or not she's selling. A move isn't an option right now."

"Then we're at a stalemate," she decided.

Looking concerned as much as guarded now, he said, "I'm going to tell Mother what the lab said. Will you be all right?"

"I'm not going to fall apart again. I'm going to help the girls finish their pictures, then we're going to get supper."

He was looking at her as if he felt sorry for her and she hated that.

Without trying to convince him that her emotions were under control, she went to the living room to be with Abby and Marianne. She needed to hold on to Abby and she needed to get to know her daughter, as well as the child she'd raised.

## Chapter Seven

Chase hunkered down to prune another vine. The early March day had almost reached the sixties. The sun was bright…the sky was blue. He and Stan had spent most of the morning replacing posts.

Something made Chase look up now, and he noticed Jillian walking toward him through the rows of trellises, Buff wandering beside her in a not-so-direct line. He remembered the expression on Jillian's face when she'd put Marianne to bed last night.

Marianne had nestled in her lap, patted her cheek and asked, "Read me a story, Jilly?"

Jillian's eyes had been full of emotion—joy at getting to know her new daughter, anguish at learning that Abby wasn't hers. The past few days had been tough for her.

Today she was wearing jeans and the green flannel jacket she'd brought from Florida. The breeze blew her hair away from her face, and even though the ground was uneven, even though she had to watch her step now and then, she walked with a grace that always caught Chase's attention.

Setting the pruning scissors on the ground and wiping his hands on his jeans, he stood. She obviously wasn't in a hurry or this didn't seem to be an emergency.

"What's up?" he asked.

Stopping before him, she summoned a smile. "Sherry called. I tried to reach you on your cell phone but it must be turned off."

"I left it in the winery office to charge. What did Sherry want? Did she change her mind about the wedding?"

With an excited yip, Buff ran to Jillian's side and stood with his paws on her jeans. Smiling, she petted him. "No. But it seems that her friend who recommended the vineyard might have had an ulterior motive."

"What motive?"

After patting Buff again, Jillian straightened. "Margaret Gorman's a reporter with the *Clarion,* and she'd like to do a comprehensive story on the vineyard and the wedding. I didn't know how you'd feel about that."

The more Chase had thought about the wedding in recent days, the more he'd wondered how much of a production it was going to be. Willow Creek would indeed be invaded with caterers, guests and florists.

"Maybe Sherry and Tom should just elope," he suggested wryly.

"Is that what you did?" Jillian asked with perception that sometimes unsettled him.

"Fran and I eloped to Vegas." His memories of his marriage to Fran were becoming dimmer, especially when he was around Jillian. He didn't like that at all. Now he conjured them up as vividly as he could. "Neither of us wanted any fuss so we flew to Nevada. Afterward, though, I was concerned Fran would regret it."

"Why?"

"It was…mechanical. Weddings are a business anywhere, I guess, but particularly there it was like an assembly line. Fran didn't complain, but then she never complained about anything. What about you? What kind of wedding did you have?"

Although he wasn't sure why, he wanted to encourage Jillian to talk about her marriage. It was important to him for her to confide in him about everything that had happened.

He thought she might not answer his question. But after a moment she responded, "We got married in front of the justice of the peace with a few friends there, and then went out to dinner afterward." Shifting the conversation back to him, she asked, "You still miss your wife, don't you?"

The missing had become less intense, especially over this past year. But that was because so much else had happened—his dad's death, moving Marianne to Willow Creek and Marianne's illness. However, his love for Fran and his memories of her still ran like a river beneath it all.

"Yes, I do miss her. How about you? Do you miss your husband?"

"I remember him," Jillian answered simply and left it at that.

Chase could only imagine how much heartache some of those memories caused if Mrs. Carmichael had been accurate concerning what happened. "Where did you go on your honeymoon?" he pushed, hoping she'd reveal *something*.

Jillian looked surprised he'd asked. "Eric could only take a few days away from his job, so we flew to New York City."

He'd seen one picture on an end table in Jillian's living room of a man her age. He wondered if she'd kept it so she could tell Abby about him. "Does Abby ever ask about him?"

Averting her gaze, Jillian let her eyes wander to the top of the maples, the acres of vines on trellises, the rolling hills. "No. I think she's still too little to realize what a family is supposed to be—a mom, a dad and children. In her playgroup she sees dads sometimes, but she hasn't asked any questions."

"Do you tell her about Eric?"

When Jillian gnawed her lower lip, he knew he was making her uncomfortable. But he wanted to shake information out of her, shake feelings out of her, shake confidences out of her. "I don't mention Eric. Abby was only fourteen months old when he died and if she has memories of him, they're probably subconscious ones."

"I've shown Marianne pictures of Fran." He knew Jillian had probably seen the picture of him and Fran in Marianne's room. "I've told her Fran was her mommy. Now explanations are going to get a lot more complicated."

Still gazing into the distance rather than at him, Jillian said, "My first thought after we got the report was we should both pretend none of this happened. We should both just go back to our lives. It would be so much easier."

"Would it, Jillian?"

Her gaze swung back to his. "I guess some people can live in denial and ignore the truth. Whenever I look at Marianne, I know I can't do that. Yet when I look at Abby, I wish I could."

His heart hurt for her…hurt for both of them. "If you moved here, you wouldn't have to stay in the house as you are now. The carriage house over by the barn could be turned into living quarters again without too much trouble."

"I'd live there with Abby?" There was some dismay in her voice.

"For a while."

"But the girls are doing everything together now. They've become inseparable."

"Instead of you and Abby living on your own, they could spend a week with you and then a week with me."

Jillian shook her head. "I don't know, Chase."

Her reticence suddenly made him angry, and he wondered what she was hoping for. "I'm not going to go away. I'm not going to say to you 'You can take the girls to Florida and I'll visit a couple of times a year.' That's not going to happen, Jillian. I want them with *me* as much as you want them with *you*."

What he saw in her face told him she had hoped for exactly that scenario.

"I should hire a lawyer," she said almost defiantly.

"Both of us will have to hire lawyers. But the bottom line is—if we don't want a judge making decisions for us, we'd better come up with something that works."

After Buff chased a robin into the sky, he sniffled the earth, then returned to Jillian. This time when he yipped and jumped up and down, she gathered him into her arms and held him close.

Chase knew both girls needed a mother, and he wouldn't think of separating them from Jillian. But he intended to be a father, too. She wasn't going to take that away from him. Besides that, the idea of his mother selling Willow Creek didn't sit well with him anymore.

While ruffling Buff's fur, Jillian set him on the ground beside a trellis post. "What should I tell Sherry and her friend?" Jillian asked, ending a discussion that seemed to have no place to go.

His objective when he'd returned to Willow Creek was to put the vineyard on the map. A story in the paper could help him do that. "Give her the go-ahead. It will be good PR, especially if she's not only going to do background but cover the wedding, too."

"I can tell you what will happen."

"What?"

"More couples will call you about having their weddings here. Is that why you're doing it? So I'll have a reason to stay?"

"Is that so distasteful for you to consider? I don't want the vineyard to become a three-ring circus. But if you could start your business here in Pennsylvania with a few weddings, it could be one solution to our problem."

She frowned. "It's not easy to start over. I did that when I moved to Florida. Building a business takes time."

"If you're worried about money, don't be. I'll cover any expenses—"

"No, you won't, Chase. I don't take handouts. I'm not going to depend on you... Not for anything."

"Don't draw that line in the sand yet," he warned her.

She was so damn independent and he'd never had to deal with that with Fran. Jillian was so damn young, too, and maybe that was part of it. She simply didn't see the bigger picture and somehow he had to show her exactly what it was.

"I'd better get back to the house. I told your mother I'd help her with supper."

"She's letting you?" he asked, trying to lighten the atmosphere a bit.

"I think she's going to agree to let me peel the potatoes."

As she turned, he clasped her shoulder. "I know you miss Florida, Jillian. I know it's not easy sharing a kitchen with another woman who wants to own it. The carriage house could be a solution."

"I'm looking for the *best* solution, Chase."

With that resolution laid before him, she walked off.

He didn't think there was a better solution. They simply had to find one they could both live with.

That evening, Jillian went to the kitchen and opened the door to the basement. She'd never been to the wine cellar. She could wait until Chase came upstairs again, but Eleanor had told her he might be in the cellar awhile.

The girls were occupied coloring and Eleanor was knitting as Jillian went down the stairs. The light was on. She descended the steps into a large open room with a concrete floor.

There were quite a few boxes stacked to the right of the stairway labeled in Chase's handwriting. One said Kitchen, another, Fran's Plates. It looked as if Chase had never unpacked.

Crossing the room, she faced a wall with a heavy

wooden door. It had a small square window near the top and she could see light inside. The door was indeed heavy as she unlatched it and pulled it open. It creaked and groaned as if it was a century old, and she realized it might be.

As she stepped onto the ground floor of the basement room, Chase ordered, "Close the door."

He was holding a clipboard, and a crate sat at his feet. Apparently he was pulling bottles of wine from the shelves.

"The temperature stays constant with the door closed," he explained.

"It's about the same temperature as in the winery."

"Yes, it is. But the winery is mechanically arranged. This is natural."

She eyed the racks of bottles. "What are you doing?"

"Selecting a few bottles from our private storehouse for a friend of mine. He's having a dinner Saturday night and asked me to come. Would you like to go with me?"

The invitation startled her for a moment. "How formal is it? I didn't bring anything dressy."

"Actually, it's casual. I'll be wearing a sweater and jeans. You can do the same."

Meeting Chase's friends for the first time, she'd want to wear something a little nicer than jeans. "What about the girls? I don't want your mother to think we're taking advantage of her."

"You'll have to find another excuse if you don't want to go. You know my mother loves to be with them. It's as if she soaks up every smile and every giggle, saving it for later."

"Don't you do that, too?" Jillian asked before she thought better of it. "Just in case…"

Awkward silence filled the chilly room. "I suppose I do," he acknowledged, a nerve working in his jaw. He saw the papers in her hand. "Did you need something?"

Of course she hadn't come down here just to see him…just to be with him. Of course she hadn't.

The aura Chase exuded always intrigued her. He was confident, sometimes with a hint of arrogance. He was sexy, no doubt about that. That brown hair falling over his brow made her want to push it back. And beyond all that, he was caring. He'd cared deeply about his wife and still loved her. He cared fiercely for Abby and Marianne. But Jillian was afraid of him in a way, and that was foolish. She had nothing to fear.

She had *everything* to fear.

She could fight him tooth and nail for Abby or for Marianne, but she had the feeling he had the power and influence she didn't have. Maybe she should go with him to see his friends so she could learn more about him, see him in action with them. Eric had managed to hide his propensity for flirting until after they were married. He'd pretended to care deeply but obviously hadn't. He'd known the words to say that would convince her to reconcile with him, but no sense of commitment had gone with them. The more she was with Chase, the more she saw him interact with others, the more she could decide exactly what his true character was. She would not be fooled a second time.

"I'll go with you Saturday night. It sounds like fun."

He didn't react and she wondered if he cared *what* she did when it didn't involve the girls.

When she moved closer to him, she held out the paper in her hand. "I have the estimate for Sherry and Tom's wedding. She wanted me to call her today, and I thought you'd like to see the figures first."

"In case we do this more than once?" he asked, pushing her to stay again.

"Let up, Chase," she said softly. "Give me some space."

He looked almost amused when he shook his head and admitted, "When I see the solution to a problem, I just want to make it happen."

"Your solution and mine might be different," she reminded him.

The amusement vanished, replaced by a piercing regard that she imagined was supposed to intimidate her. It didn't. She'd learned how to stand up for herself and her daughter, and she'd do that no matter what.

Finally, he took the paper from her hand and examined it closely. "This looks reasonable to me. You *are* going to take a commission out of this, aren't you?"

"That's figured in. Are you sure you don't want to charge Sherry and Tom more for using the vineyard?"

"No. Especially with the print publicity we'll be getting, this is fine. You're a sharp businesswoman, Jillian, I can tell that from what you've done here."

Did he really believe that or was he saying it to flatter her?

Somehow he seemed to read her mind because he took a step closer and put his hand on her shoulder. "I mean it. I can see why you're successful at what you do."

"Kara is a big part of that," she said honestly. "In D.C. it was difficult making a name for myself. With

Kara already established in Daytona, it was easy making our business a success."

"We don't have a multitude of event planners in this area. I think you'd be able to make a name for yourself quickly. In fact, the right word in the right circles would guarantee it. My mother could go a long way with helping you with that."

"Your mother?"

"I know she doesn't seem particularly social, but she meets with her friends a few times a month. They're influential friends and word gets out. If that's what you want, I'm sure she could help."

If that's what she wanted. At this point, all she knew about what she wanted was that she didn't want to be separated from Marianne *or* Abby.

There was something clandestinely intimate about being in the wine cellar with Chase. It didn't seem like a cellar at all, not in the usual sense. The walls were some kind of gray stone with mortar in between. The ambience of the place told her it had been here for a century, maybe more. The wrought-iron light fixtures looked rustically old but they held chandelier bulbs and without turning her full attention on them, they gave the illusion of candles flickering. There was an aroma— aged bottles, old cork, Chase's aftershave.

The way he was looking at her made her tremble inside and when he took a step closer, she wanted to forget about everything going on in their lives. She wanted to be in the moment and just let whatever happened happen. All throughout her life she'd thought about her tomorrows, planned for them, tried to be prepared for whatever would come. She'd learned to do that because she and her mom had lived on a shoestring, and they could never depend on her father.

She didn't want to depend on Chase now, either. She just wanted to kiss him.

When he eased closer, she found herself mesmerized by the moment...mesmerized by him.

"It would be better for us and the girls if we were friends and not enemies." His voice was low and intimately husky.

"Friends?" she asked, wondering what he meant by the word.

"There are all kinds of friends, Jillian. Maybe we can explore the idea."

Explore? The idea of exploration with Chase seemed monumental...exciting...bone-melting.

When his hand slipped under her hair, she looked up at him, the turmoil of everything they'd been through roiling inside of her.

"There's something hot between us," he said as he bent his head. "Maybe we both need to forget about everything else but that. This might be reckless," he murmured, right before his lips touched hers, "but I'm feeling reckless right now."

The last time she was reckless, she'd let Eric charm her. The last time she was reckless...

Chase's kiss wasn't hot, it was blazing. It burned away everything but the two of them and enclosed them in a world away. When his other arm went around her, she let the estimate sheet float to the floor. His hold was possessive as if he were claiming her somehow. His kiss became demanding as if now were the only moment they had and it was all that mattered. She found herself swept away by Chase...swept into his passion. Desire had been foreign to her for so long. She hadn't even allowed herself to think about attraction to anyone.

But keeping a tight rein on her restraint and control wasn't an option when it came to Chase. He surrounded her as his tongue filled her mouth, taunted expertly, thrust inside seductively. They seemed to fit together perfectly, and she felt the adventure of exploration.

Engrossed in the kiss, Chase's taste, the scent of male and aftershave and desire, she hardly noticed when he shifted, when his hand went to her waist, when his long deft fingers eased under her sweater. As she felt the scalding touch of his skin against hers, her breath hitched and her soft throaty moan sounded deep inside of her. She knew she should stop him, stop this, stop everything. They weren't friends, not with the tangled knot of complications between them. But she felt powerless to end something so exquisite…to end sensations she'd never felt before, and passion that curled into her deepest secret womanly place. For all his expertise, Eric's satisfaction had always come first. Now she longed to find out what kind of lover Chase would be.

As his tongue retreated for a few moments and he nipped her upper lip, his hand moved higher and she knew his target. He moved slowly, and the anticipation thrilled her almost as much as the thought of what he wanted to do.

"I want to touch you, Jillian. It's been a long time since I touched a woman like this."

"It's been a long time for me, too," she murmured.

Their words to each other had been soft, but suddenly she heard them again, very loud, as if they were echoing in the cavern.

*It's been a long time since I touched a woman like this.*
*It's been a long time for me, too.*

They weren't in the wine cellar alone. Ghosts from their pasts dogged them. She'd thought living in the moment would be a solution, would be a distraction, would be a pleasure. Yet now she knew it couldn't be. She never engaged in sex lightly, not without a relationship. There had been one man before Eric—her first love, who had moved on after he'd gone to college. That had been the total extent of her experience.

And Chase? He still loved his wife. That was obvious. What was she doing? What did she expect to come of this except trouble?

When she leaned away, Chase moved his hand from under her sweater, his gaze on hers.

"What's wrong?" he asked, his voice husky.

She knew that he already knew. "This isn't the way to become friends. We'll mess everything up."

"It's not in a mess now?" he asked wryly.

"You know what I mean. I don't even trust you, and—"

"Why don't you trust me?" he interrupted.

She shook her head.

"How can we be friends when you won't tell me anything about yourself?"

Hearing his frustration, she answered quickly, "You already know a lot about me."

"I know a few facts. I know you're a good mother."

"I'm confused, Chase, aren't you? I have so many decisions to make and I don't want to make them because you—"

"I what?" he asked warily.

"Because you manipulated me into making them."

Now he took a step back and his tone was defensive. "I don't use manipulation."

"You want me to move my life here. You want to get your own way. Why wouldn't you use this…attraction between us to do that?"

"Because I'm not that kind of man," he said angrily.

She didn't know if he was or he wasn't. That was the whole crux of the problem. Until she found out, she'd better watch her step. Caution had served her well since her move to Florida. She wasn't going to throw it to the wind now.

"We don't know each other, Chase, but we're going to be tied to each other until the girls are grown. Let's keep this simple."

He gave a humorless laugh. "Take off the rose-colored glasses, Jillian. You won't find 'simple' between *us*."

"Maybe you're right."

He was silent for a long time. Finally he stooped, picked up the estimate sheet and held it out to her. "What about Saturday night?"

"Do you still want me to go?"

"I want you to go," he answered.

Taking the paper from him, she said, "I'll meet your friends."

Before she left, she had to be sure of something. "Are you certain you want to have this wedding here?"

He didn't hesitate. "I'm certain. Once I make up my mind, I don't change it."

She didn't know if his words were meant to be reassuring or if they were meant to warn her. Deciding the wine cellar now seemed dangerous instead of intimate,

# The Silhouette Reader Service™ — Here's how it works:

Accepting your 2 free books and gift places you under no obligation to buy anything. You may keep the books and gift and return the shipping statement marked "cancel." If you do not cancel, about a month later we'll send you 6 additional books and bill you just $4.24 each in the U.S., or $4.99 each in Canada, plus 25¢ shipping & handling per book and applicable taxes if any.* That's the complete price and — compared to cover prices of $4.99 each in the U.S. and $5.99 each in Canada — it's quite a bargain! You may cancel at any time, but if you choose to continue, every month we'll send you 6 more books, which you may either purchase at the discount price or return to us and cancel your subscription.
*Terms and prices subject to change without notice. Sales tax applicable in N.Y. Canadian residents will be charged applicable provincial taxes and GST. Credit or debit balances in a customer's account(s) may be offset by any other outstanding balance owed by or to the customer.

If offer card is missing write to: Silhouette Reader Service, 3010 Walden Ave., P.O. Box 1867, Buffalo NY 14240-1867

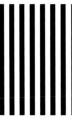

NO POSTAGE
NECESSARY
IF MAILED
IN THE
UNITED STATES

## BUSINESS REPLY MAIL
FIRST-CLASS MAIL    PERMIT NO. 717-003    BUFFALO, NY

POSTAGE WILL BE PAID BY ADDRESSEE

SILHOUETTE READER SERVICE
3010 WALDEN AVE
PO BOX 1867
BUFFALO NY 14240-9952

# GET FREE BOOKS and a FREE GIFT WHEN YOU PLAY THE...

## SLOT MACHINE GAME!

*Just scratch off the silver box with a coin. Then check below to see the gifts you get!*

# YES! I have scratched off the silver box. Please send me the 2 free Silhouette Special Edition® books and gift for which I qualify. I understand I am under no obligation to purchase any books, as explained on the back of this card.

## 335 SDL D354                                    235 SDL D36L

| FIRST NAME | LAST NAME |

ADDRESS

| APT.# | CITY |

| STATE/PROV. | ZIP/POSTAL CODE |

| 7 7 7 | **Worth TWO FREE BOOKS plus a BONUS Mystery Gift!** |
| 🍒 🍒 🍒 | **Worth TWO FREE BOOKS!** |
| ♣ ♣ ♣ | **Worth ONE FREE BOOK!** |
| 🔔 🔔 🍒 | **TRY AGAIN!** |

www.eHarlequin.com

(S-SE-12/04)

DETACH AND MAIL CARD TODAY!

she crossed to the heavy door and opened it. When she pushed the portal shut behind her, she felt relief…and disappointment.

Maybe on Saturday night she could get a better handle on Chase. Maybe after Saturday night, she could decide whether a move to Pennsylvania would be in her and Abby's and Marianne's best interest.

## Chapter Eight

The dinner party was in full swing when Chase and Jillian arrived at the Paxtons' house. After Alissa Paxton took their coats she whispered to Jillian, "Everyone calls me Allie."

Chase saw Jillian's first real smile of the evening. She looked beautiful tonight. She was wearing black slacks, a soft white sweater and a black crocheted shawl casually draped over one shoulder and tied on the other. She was so classy and it didn't take him long to notice that she didn't need his presence by her side to make her feel comfortable. Obviously a mingler, she was soon involved in more than one conversation with the two other couples the Paxtons had invited, the Forsythes and the Stantons.

Ever since their encounter in the wine cellar, she'd kept to herself and so had he. He was still reeling from the fact that he'd let baser desires overtake him. All she had to do was walk into a room and he didn't know left side of his brain from his right. He didn't understand why his libido was stronger than his intelligence when it never had been before.

And then there was the guilt that his heart still belonged somewhere else even though his body desired Jillian.

Her belief that he was trying to manipulate her, the truth that she didn't trust him, disconcerted him more than he wanted to admit. Yet he understood both. If her husband had been unfaithful, if she'd been lied to, it would be difficult for her to trust again.

Was he as honest with himself? He had to admit that the desire between them was an instrument he *could* use to convince her to stay.

After an hour of conversation and hors d'oeuvres, Allie guided everyone to their seats at the dining room table.

Before they began the meal, Chase produced two bottles of wine. To everyone he suggested, "Let's start with the Niagara. Tell me what you think."

It seemed odd, but Jillian hadn't yet sampled Willow Creek wines.

Chase first poured the white wine for everyone and watched as Jillian took a sip and savored it on her tongue. He could tell from her smile and pleased expression that she liked it.

"Too grapey for me," Scott commented.

But Allie joked, "You like wine so dry the taste will last on your tongue for a week."

Everyone laughed.

When Chase poured from the second bottle—a

Chardonnay—*that* was more to Scott's liking. Soon everyone was enjoying the wine of their choice with the meal.

Carly Forsythe, who was a pretty blonde around Chase's age and seated to Jillian's right, remarked, "Greg told me you and Scott and James are planning a camping trip in May into the Appalachians. He's already started to buy gear. You *do* know you won't get any sleep for as long as you're gone. His snoring will echo through the mountains."

Scott slapped Greg on the back. "Your secret's out."

Laughter spread around the table.

The four of them had discussed the trip a few months ago but everything had been different then. "I'm not sure I'll be able to go," Chase informed them, exchanging a look with Scott. He knew his friend would understand.

"Not go?" Greg bellowed. "Of course you'll go. Those vines aren't going to wither and die because you go away for a week."

"It's more complicated than that," Chase said matter-of-factly. "I need to keep my eye on Marianne."

"I thought you said they repaired her heart and she's doing fine," James Stanton said.

"She is right now, but there's a lot going on."

"Why don't you tell them," Scott murmured. "It's all going to come out eventually. Shouldn't your friends be the first to know?"

With a glance at Jillian, Chase saw she looked horrified. But this was *his* decision to make. He'd known the guys and two of the women since high school. When he'd played football, Allie and James's wife, Trish, had been cheerleaders. Scott had been on the team, and

James and Greg had always been around, ready for any prank or escapade they could think up.

Everyone would know eventually.

All eyes were on him now, including Jillian's. Hers were a bit pleading but he'd had enough of keeping facts hidden. He'd had enough of lies even if they were well meant.

"Before Marianne's surgery, I discovered I'm not her father."

Trish gasped.

Carly's mouth rounded in an *O*.

James and Greg looked stunned.

As quickly and simply as he could, he explained what had happened. Then all eyes turned to Jillian. "You must be devastated," Carly said.

Trish was shaking her head. "I just can't imagine it. Didn't you say you lived in Florida? What are you going to do?"

Jillian looked shell-shocked for about half a minute. Then in that way she had of composing herself, her shoulders squared, her chin lifted, and she told Chase's friends, "I'm not sure yet. I haven't worked it all out. It hasn't been that long since the DNA results came in."

"My goodness," Trish said. "What an awful mistake. Are you going to tell Marianne and…Abby, is it?"

"Eventually."

"If you switch them back, or even if both of them live with one of you half a year, you're going to have to explain something to them. Are you going to sue the hospital?" James asked.

"That hasn't even come up," Chase responded. "It wouldn't help our situation any."

James added with a weak smile, "Maybe not. But you could pay for the girls' education that way."

Suddenly standing, Jillian pushed back her chair. "If you'll excuse me, I'm going to freshen up before dessert." In the calm graceful way she had, she left the room, and Chase knew he had to go after her.

Leaving the others still discussing the idea of a lawsuit, he caught up to her in the hallway that led to the powder room.

When he clasped her elbow, she wrenched away from him. "I don't want to talk, Chase."

"Everyone is going to find out eventually."

"Everyone? Who is everyone? Are you going to make an announcement everywhere you go?"

"Be reasonable about this. These are my friends."

"The least you could have done was let me know you had told Scott. I might have been more prepared."

"I've known him since high school, Jillian. We talked after I found out my blood type wasn't compatible with Marianne's. *You* told Kara. What's the difference?"

"I knew Kara wouldn't spread it all over Daytona Beach."

"The real problem here is—you haven't accepted this yet. You have *not* accepted the fact that Marianne is your daughter and Abby is mine."

"Why are you able to accept this so easily?" she wanted to know, and now the anger was gone from her voice.

"Easily? Is that what it looks like to you? Every time I look at Marianne, I feel torn up inside. Every time I look at Abby, I think about the three years I've missed with her. Nothing about this is easy. But I'm a pragmatist. It is what it is, and we have to deal with it. So you'd better take your head out of the sand and face reality."

Looking at her, the sadness in her eyes, the love she had for Abby that she thought she had to let go of, he wanted to take her in his arms. Every time his elbow had brushed hers at dinner, his knee had grazed hers, his breath had inhaled her perfume, desire had stirred and reminded him of his body's needs.

There was something in Jillian's eyes he couldn't name—distrust, suspicion, anguish, maybe even resignation?

He saw her take a bolstering breath and then she said, "Go back to your friends, Chase. I need a few minutes to myself."

Slipping into the powder room, she locked the door.

He'd thought tonight would give them a break from their problems. He'd thought tonight would neutralize the situation between them. He couldn't have been more wrong.

It was almost midnight when Jillian and Chase returned home. The lights were blazing in the downstairs of the house and Stan's truck was parked in front of the garage.

"Chase—" Jillian couldn't finish, worried something had happened to the girls. She unbuckled her seat belt quickly and rushed out of Chase's sedan.

In a moment he was beside her. He opened the door, and they went down the hall to the kitchen. "Mother would have called us if anything was wrong," he decided, but there was worry in his tone.

When they reached the kitchen, they found Eleanor seated at the table, a blanket around her shoulders.

The microwave beeped and Stan took a mug from inside, dropping a tea bag into it.

"What's going on?" Chase asked, eyeing his uncle and his mother.

Sliding out of her coat, Jillian hung it on a hook, noticing how gray Eleanor looked.

"She has a fever of one hundred and two degrees and a sore throat. When she felt woozy, she called me."

Chase went over to his mother, pulled out a chair in front of her and sat down.

"Did you feel poorly before we left?"

"My throat was a little scratchy, that's all," she said in a croak. "Later, I felt dizzy and afraid I'd pass out with the girls. Stan came over to put them to bed."

"Why didn't you call us?" Jillian asked.

Eleanor gave a little shrug and winced as if the motion hurt. "I didn't want to interrupt your evening. It wasn't as if something was wrong with the girls."

An expression crossed Chase's face and Jillian wondered what he was thinking. He said in a clear, low voice, "You're as important as the girls."

Tears welled up in Eleanor's eyes, and Jillian wondered if she was feeling that poorly or if something else was going on here that Jillian didn't understand.

After a few moments of awkward silence, Stan stepped in, plunking down the mug of tea on the table beside Eleanor. "She needs to be in bed. She's always waiting on everybody else. Now she needs to be taken care of."

Eleanor laid a calming hand on Stan's arm. "Don't be silly. I'll be fine in the morning."

"I doubt that," Stan retorted, "but I know better than

anyone that you've got a mind of your own. Since reinforcements have arrived, I'll head out."

At the door, Eleanor stopped him with, "Thank you."

"Don't mention it," he mumbled, then hurried down the hall and out the door.

"He's a good man," Eleanor said pensively, looking after him.

"He's right about one thing," Chase said, rising to his feet. "You need to be in bed. Let me help you upstairs."

"I'll bring your tea and maybe a glass of juice. Vitamin C might help," Jillian added.

"Apple juice, not orange," Eleanor demanded. "Apple won't hurt my throat."

Jillian almost smiled. Eleanor would have her way, one way or the other.

After Chase helped his mother to her bedroom, keeping his hand on her elbow to steady her, Jillian offered, "If you want to check on the girls, I'll stay and help your mom."

"I'll be back shortly." He gave his mother another concerned look.

"Don't worry, Chase. Tomorrow I'll be fine," Eleanor said.

"I'll bring one of the monitors in here and if you need anything, all you have to do is say so."

When he left the room, Eleanor mumbled, "Always thinks he knows best. I'll keep it turned off."

The evening had been emotionally draining for Jillian. After she had gone back to the dinner party, everyone had acted as if they'd hadn't been trampling in her private life. Eleanor's gruffness now was an endearing distraction. The older lady didn't like being the center of attention and, like everyone else, she wanted her own way.

"Chase just wants to make sure you're taken care of."

When Eleanor lifted her gaze to Jillian's, Jillian saw pain there and didn't understand it.

"He has enough on his hands with the winery and Marianne and…Abby."

Jillian didn't react to that, just pulled back the covers on the bed. "I'll check on you before I go downstairs in the morning, if that's okay. I can fix breakfast."

When Eleanor pulled the blanket tighter around her, Jillian could see a shiver go through the older woman. "Would you like me to get your nightgown for you?"

"Middle dresser drawer," Eleanor said, holding the blanket tight.

After Jillian took a blue flannel nightgown from the drawer, she laid it on the bed. "Would you like me to leave while you get ready?"

Eleanor eyed her and then said, "No need for that. When I joined the tennis club I had to get used to locker rooms."

"You play tennis?"

"I did for years, but I had to stop a few years back. Arthritis in my shoulder. I miss it."

"I bet you do. Are you doing anything in place of it?"

"I still ride Giselle," Eleanor said, referring to her mare. "*You* look good on a horse. Did you ride much in Florida?"

"A little. I'm no expert but I can make a horse go where I want him to. When I was a teenager, a friend of mine had a farm. Her dad would lead us on a trail ride every once in a while, but I always had an old horse that just followed along."

"Chase rides most mornings. You should go along."

Jillian had only been out riding a few times in the afternoon when the girls were napping. She realized she'd like to ride with Chase sometime.

In a few moments, Eleanor had thrown off the blanket, undressed and changed into her nightgown, then slipped into the bed and pulled up the covers. "Chase said you grew up in Vermont. I hear it's beautiful there."

"It is, but it's beautiful here, too."

"Are your parents living?"

"My mother's gone. After she died, I had to sell the house in Vermont."

"And your father?"

"I have no idea where he is. I had an address for him when I graduated from college, but he didn't come to my graduation and after that, every letter I wrote to him was returned."

"Your parents were divorced?"

Jillian nodded. "When I was eight."

"Divorce is probably something a child never quite gets over," Eleanor decided. "That's why I would never consider one."

Thinking about Eric and what had happened between them, Jillian returned, "Sometimes there's no choice."

Although Eleanor hunkered down under the covers, she gave Jillian a long, penetrating look. "You and your husband had problems?"

There was no point in stalling her. "Yes." Since Jillian didn't want to have that conversation, she asked, "Is there anything else you need? Anything I can get you?"

Eleanor shook her head. "Leave the night-light on in the hall and I'll be fine."

When Jillian went to the door, she said, "I'm sure Chase will bring in the monitor soon."

Jillian was pulling the door part way shut when Eleanor asked, "Are you going to stay in Pennsylvania?"

Jillian had told herself she hadn't made up her mind, but now she said, "I can't imagine leaving either of my daughters," and on that she went out into the hall, not wanting to be questioned further.

If she moved her life to Pennsylvania, would the Remmingtons become her extended family?

If she moved her life to Pennsylvania, would she want them to?

Much to Eleanor's dismay, she was still under the weather the next day. When Jillian brought her meals, Abby and Marianne were close by. However, Chase had ordered them not to go into Eleanor's room. He didn't want Marianne picking up a virus while she was recuperating. So Marianne and Abby stood outside the door, peeking in, giggling and waving.

Midafternoon, Chase returned to the house to check on Eleanor and found the girls in the living room with Jillian. She'd just finished putting Marianne's hair in pigtails like Abby's though the pigtails were much stubbier because her hair was shorter.

"Daddy, Daddy. I have tails," she said with excited glee as Chase came into the room.

"I see you've got tails." He smiled and suggested to Jillian, "It's a beautiful day out there. I thought they might want to walk over to the barn."

"I wanna wide Pwancer," Abby stated, picking up on their conversation.

It had been over three weeks since Marianne's surgery and at her doctor's appointment a few days before, he'd lifted restrictions. She'd passed her last echocardiogram with flying colors. Still, Jillian didn't know if Chase would want her riding. And if Abby did…

"I don't know, Bitsy-bug. Maybe you can just pat Prancer," Jillian suggested to Abby.

Marianne looked up at her dad with a frown. "I don' wanna ride."

Jillian knew Marianne was afraid of horses, including her Shetland pony, Prancer.

Crossing to Abby, Chase lifted her up high until she giggled. "You can sit on Prancer and Marianne can watch."

"I don' wanna ride Prancer," Marianne repeated adamantly, shaking her head.

"You can get as close as you want," Chase assured her. "I'll take a few carrots along and we can give them all a snack."

Jillian had seen the look in Chase's eyes when he picked up Abby. He wanted to claim her, Jillian could tell, but the girls weren't old enough to understand.

She noticed Chase watched Marianne as they made their way to the barn. She jabbered at Abby, stooped to pat Buff and skipped a few steps.

"She's going to be fine," Jillian assured him.

"I've been worried about her since she was born. It's hard to let go of that."

The sun was dazzling, the air redolent with pine and new leaves and warm earth. As they walked to the lower level of the barn, Jillian saw how Chase seemed to be a part of all of it. He was wearing jeans and a black T-shirt today. His upper arms were muscled, his body fit and trim and powerful-looking. He belonged here, and she couldn't understand why it had taken him so long to return.

Abby wanted to feed the horses carrots and Marianne wanted no part of that, either. Chase broke the carrots in half, and lifted Abby so she could feed the mare Eleanor rode and, with a little coaxing, the Appaloosa he took on trail rides. Marianne stayed close to Jillian's side, away from the stalls that opened into the corral. At first Abby giggled as Chase's horse, Desperado, nuzzled her hand. Then she said so fast it was hard to catch, "I wanna wide Pwancer *now.*"

Chase set her down. "All right. Let me get a saddle."

Prancer was a brown Shetland with a black mane. He had a sweet disposition and stood fairly still as Chase positioned the blanket on his back and then cinched the girth on the saddle. Abby had no fear of the pony and while Chase was readying him, she was petting his nose, running her fingers through his mane and laying her head against his chest.

"Nice pon-ee," she crooned.

With avid curiosity, Marianne watched it all. After Chase lifted Abby into the saddle, he took the lead and walked her around the corral.

She laughed. "See, Mommy! See, Mommy!"

"I see." Jillian didn't want Marianne to feel left out so she picked her up and held her as Buff snuffled the long grass at the fence. Finally Abby had enough and Chase began to lead the pony and rider back to the barn once more.

"I wanna pet him," Marianne whispered close to Jillian's ear.

"You do?" Jillian was surprised and then realized Abby's ease with the animals must have had an effect.

Marianne nodded.

"Do you want me to hold you?" Jillian asked as they approached the horse.

When Marianne shook her head, Jillian set her on the ground.

With Abby sitting in the saddle, and Chase holding the head so the horse didn't move, Marianne went up to Prancer and stood two feet away. They all waited.

"Try his neck," Chase encouraged her.

Tentatively, Marianne reached up and her fingers briefly touched his coat. She giggled and pulled her hand back.

"Go ahead, honey," Jillian encouraged her. "You can touch his mane, too."

A little bolder this time, Marianne slid her fingers down a strand of the horse's mane as Prancer lowered his head, then rubbed her palm against his neck. Laughing, she decided, "He's fuzz-ee."

After a few more pats, Jillian crouched down with her and held Marianne's hand to the pony's nose. She laughed all over again when she felt how soft it was.

When Prancer swished his tail at a fly and lifted his head, Marianne had had enough. Backing away, she said, "I'm gonna play wif Buff now."

A few minutes later, the girls were playing hide-and-seek with Buff around the hay bales in the barn while Chase groomed Prancer.

Jillian asked, "Anything I can do to help?"

"This will only take a few minutes."

Jillian couldn't be idle, though. Finding another

brush with the tack in the corner of the barn, she stood on the other side of Prancer, grooming him, too.

Every once in a while, her hand got tangled up with Chase's and they'd gaze into each other's eyes for a long moment. She didn't know what to say or do or how to act with him. If she just kept her hands busy...

"You and Abby are good for Marianne," he said. "She hasn't gone near that pony since I bought him for her. I think Abby's going to teach her how to be adventurous."

"I'm not sure that's a good thing," Jillian warned him.

He laughed. "Marianne told me you made pancakes for her this morning. Pancakes with a face."

"Just blueberries and a banana nose. Your mother was impressed, too," she joked. His lingering smile made her stomach turn upside down.

"My mother isn't used to being taken care of. She doesn't usually let anyone attempt it."

"She didn't feel well and her defenses were down."

Looking over her shoulder, Jillian saw Abby hiding between two hay bales with Buff while Marianne tried to find them.

"Why did you leave and not come back for so very long?" she asked. She knew it was a personal question, and she also knew he might brush it off.

However, after paying particular attention to grooming Prancer's withers, Chase answered curtly, "I didn't come back because of my father."

"Your mother said you idolized him, that you followed him everywhere when you were a boy and that's how you got interested in wine-making."

"I did idolize him. I thought he was the epitome of what a man should be. Then I found out he wasn't. He and I had differences we couldn't conquer. I couldn't work with him when I didn't respect him, and that's why my life took a different course."

"What could have—?"

"I don't like talking about my father any more than you like talking about your marriage. Or has that changed?"

They were both holding back. He wanted her to trust him and she couldn't. Until she did, it was obvious he wasn't going to open up to her. Maybe that was for the best.

"I see it hasn't." His voice was gruff.

Checking his watch, he said, "The reporter from the *Clarion* is going to be here in about fifteen minutes. She called me this morning. I've also gotten two more calls about having weddings here. Sherry and Tom must be spreading the word."

"What did you tell everyone?" Jillian asked.

"I told them I'd get back to them. Are you interested?"

With a few weddings, with an article in the newspaper which would probably lead to more business, Jillian knew she could get a foothold in this area. She was good at what she did and word would spread. It was time to get off the fence and decide where her new life was headed, a new life with two daughters if she had anything to say about it.

"Are you sure you want Willow Creek to become a venue for weddings?"

"If it means you'll stay here in Pennsylvania, weddings are fine with me. I'll work around them."

"I can't leave Abby or Marianne, so moving here does seem to be the best solution. But I'm probably going to have to fly to Florida a few times to tie up things there. I've spoken to Kara about it and she understands."

After he canvassed her face for a long moment, he nodded. "You're making the right decision, Jillian."

She didn't know if she was, but she did know leaving either of the girls wasn't an option. If she had to call Pennsylvania her new home, so be it.

And if she had to co-parent with Chase?

She'd watch her back, every step of the way.

## Chapter Nine

When Chase came in the back door of the kitchen the following morning, he saw his mother sitting at the table with papers strewn in front of her. She was feeling better now and had taken over cooking meals again. However, she was letting Jillian pitch in, too.

Jillian.

With her agreeing to move to Pennsylvania, they'd taken care of one very big hurdle in parenting Marianne and Abby. But there were still more hurdles, and he intended to demolish those, too.

Going to the sink, he washed up. Spring weather seemed to have taken hold. Willow Creek's seasonal workers were back on the grounds now, and he was overseeing for the most part.

Drying his hands on the towel, he glanced at the papers on the table. "What's all this? Notes for the wine appreciation class you're giving?"

"No, though I do have to get ready for that since it's happening this weekend. About twenty-five people signed up."

She picked up a business card and studied it. "These are documents a real estate agent gave me. Properties comparable to Willow Creek and what we could get for it. Stan thinks I should sell, that I'm getting too old for all the hassle. How would you feel if I did?"

When Chase had returned to Willow Creek he'd never expected it to be a permanent move, but he was enjoying the work as he used to when he was a teenager. He knew he could win awards with Willow Creek wines just as his dad had done years before when the wine-making process was all-important to him. Jillian and the girls seemed to like it here. When he was outside working, he could hear their laughter as they played. He was surprised Stan had suggested his mother sell it since it had been so much a part of her life.

"If you consider selling Willow Creek, I'll buy it myself and give you the best price you could possibly get."

At that, Eleanor's gaze met his and she studied him for a long time. "I've always loved Willow Creek as much as you have, and I've always wanted it to be your legacy. I know we haven't talked about this in years, but in spite of what you think, in spite of what you feel about me, I have always loved you as a true son."

"Mother—"

"Let me finish. Your father loved you, too. That's why he married me, so you could have a stable childhood. Why haven't you been able to forgive us for caring about you so much? All we wanted to do was to protect you and give you the security every child should have."

Knowing the time had come to set things right with his mother, he sat down across from her. "Do you understand how furious I was with both you and Dad for lying to me all those years?"

The severity of her face seemed to soften. "Oh, I understood. Do you understand how hurt I was that your father could never love me with his whole heart, but that I loved you *both* that way?"

He'd known his father had hurt her. That was obvious in the distance that had always been between them. But he'd never really realized how much he had hurt her himself. He'd been selfish in that because he'd only considered the lies and how they'd made him feel. "I should have let go of my resentment over the whole situation long ago, before Dad died."

"Yes, you should have. But you didn't. However, I don't think it's ever too late. I believe your father knows what's in your heart and that you *do* love him. He disappointed you. *I* disappointed you."

"It wasn't just disappointment. When I found out the truth, suddenly I became this duty and responsibility that you'd taken on. Yes, you'd loved Dad, but you accepted me because of *him*."

"That's not true, Chase! Is that what you've been thinking all these years? My Lord, if it hadn't been for *you,* I might not have married Preston."

Chase felt as if he'd been punched in the gut. "I don't understand."

"I knew Preston loved Doreen. I knew he thought she was his one great love. But I couldn't have children."

After a few moments hesitation her cheeks reddened a bit as she confided, "As a young adult, I'd used an IUD and there was scarring. Your father knew that. He knew a baby was the best gift he could ever give me. *You* were that gift, Chase. *You* were the reason I married your father."

There had been a barrier between him and his mother ever since he'd gone off to college. The secret had made him feel disconnected. Now looking back at his childhood, looking back at the way she'd always treated him with love, not with duty, he realized he'd done her a grave injustice.

He reached out and covered her hand. "I'm sorry I stayed away for so long. Do you know when I sat across from Doreen Edwards and saw the resemblance between us, all I could think about was that she was a stranger to me and *you* were my real mother? You always were and you always will be."

Tears came to his mother's eyes. "You don't have to buy Willow Creek. It will be your inheritance. But now that Jillian has decided to move to Pennsylvania, certainly she'll want a place of her own."

"I've offered her the carriage house."

"That place is a mess. There's old furniture in there as well as old tools. And the plaster is cracked. We've had the water turned off for a while and it would need a heating system."

"All that could be taken care of. It would be worth it to keep the girls here together on this property."

"They would stay with Jillian?"

"No. I want equal access."

"She won't be happy about that."

"Neither of us are going to be completely happy in this situation."

Blinking away her tears and settling into her composed self, Eleanor said, "By the way, a reporter called...Margaret Gorman. She said the story's going to run this weekend. She decided to do it in two parts, the first part now, the second part after the wedding."

"That's fine with me."

"Did you know Jillian's been up 'til one or two the past few nights? She's been working on those wedding plans after the girls go to sleep."

"I wonder if starting up a business again here will be too much for her, now that there are two girls to look after."

"I'm sure she won't admit it if it *is* too much. She has a spine, that girl does."

Something about his mother's comment made Chase ask, "And you didn't think Fran did?"

Eleanor didn't pretend not to be making comparisons. "Remember, I only met Fran twice, once when you married and those few days you visited after she was pregnant."

"And?" Chase prompted.

"And she was a very nice lady, but she was...bland. She didn't challenge you. She didn't stand up to you. With Jillian, when she knows what she wants, she goes after it. She's not afraid to tell you exactly what she thinks...or me, either. In *my* book, that's a good thing."

"Where is she?"

"In the living room teaching the girls some kind of number songs. I suppose I'll have to learn them, too."

His mother's voice was a bit dismayed, yet he saw

the glint of amusement in her eyes. She might complain about learning kids' songs, but she was going to enjoy every minute of it.

He thought about joining Jillian and the girls. He thought about Jillian's heart-shaped face, her soft hair, her curvy figure, the remembrance of kisses that woke him in the middle of the night...and he decided he'd go back out to the winery instead. He and Jillian were too combustible, and somehow he had to learn how to handle the blaze and keep it banked so that Marianne and Abby came first.

Over the following week, Chase found Jillian consulting with him often about Sherry and Tom's wedding. Her questions were legitimate, and he knew she needed his opinion so he could tell her if what she wanted to do would interfere with the running of the winery. However, this additional contact, in the office, in the wine-tasting room or even outside without the buffer of tiny chaperones or his mother, reminded him how much he wanted to kiss her again, reminded him hunger was a moment away, reminded him he was a man with needs though he'd shoved them aside for a good long time.

Even at other times, she seemed to be everywhere in his life—on the phone in the living room with the caterer, helping his mother in the kitchen, just outside his line of vision playing with the girls and Buff. Her cell phone rang often now and most of the time it was Sherry and he realized how obsessive brides today could be, simple wedding or not.

On Sunday morning, he brought the weekend newspaper inside. Jillian was making pancakes, looking beautiful with her hair long, wavy and flowing around her face, looking sexy with her baby-blue sweater and leggings hugging every curve. He ignored the arousal that demanded his attention and sat at the table, concentrating on the paper.

It wasn't long, however, until he came to the Style section and stopped short. First he looked at the pictures. Some were those he had shown Sherry with the gardens in full bloom. Another was a long shot of Willow Creek with the house and winery. A closeup of the winery itself was paired with the history of the vineyard. The story, based on questions the reporter had asked Chase, was well written.

The only aspect of the article he didn't like was his picture staring back at him. He recognized the photo. The reporter had done her homework. It had been published in a D.C. paper when he'd won an award.

"We made the Sunday edition," he said matter-of-factly over the girls' laughter and Jillian's sweet voice.

Immediately, Jillian was by his side looking over his shoulder, pancake turner in hand. Her hair almost brushed his cheek as she leaned forward. She smelled like pancakes mixed with flowers, and his gut turned. That wasn't from hunger—at least not hunger for breakfast.

"The photos are good," she decided as she skimmed the article. "Is all of it accurate?"

As he leaned away from her, his voice was brusque. "Accurate enough."

When she glanced at him, he held her gaze, filled with the desire to hold her. When she licked her lips, he practically groaned. They glistened from that bit of moisture from her tongue, and he thought about tasting her again.

Eleanor crossed to Jillian and took the pancake turner from her hand. "They'll burn," she said with a straight face. There was a twinkle in his mother's eye that Chase hadn't seen there before.

Flustered now, her cheeks flushed, Jillian said, "This article is a public relations consultant's dream."

He thought about the dream he'd had last night of Jillian and what they'd been doing in his bed. "I didn't expect the paper to give it quite this much space."

"Did you give her your photo?"

"No. But it was in the public domain. A photographer from a D.C. paper had taken it." To change that subject, he advised, "You're going to have to come up with a name for your new business."

"I suppose so. She names me as the event planner for the wedding, but…"

The phone rang then, and Chase was glad for the distraction. "I'll get it," he said, pushing back his chair and moving away from temptation.

A few minutes later, he was crooking his finger at Jillian and holding his hand over the phone. "Someone read the article in the paper and they want you."

"Me?"

"You plan weddings, don't you?" he asked, amused.

"I guess that might become my specialty."

By that evening, Chase was no longer amused. He was ready to turn off the damn phone! The winery had an answering machine and a recording about hours and services. But the women who had called had been persistent. They'd found the residence for Willow Creek and they'd wanted to know how to get in touch with Jillian Kendall. Jillian had been on and off the phone all day. As of tonight, there were six more weddings scheduled at Willow Creek. He was going to be surrounded by flowers and tuxedos and jittery brides for the summer. He felt invaded, much too bothered by Jillian being relatively close by and in dire need of a night ride on Desperado.

During dinner, there was yet another call. After Jillian returned to the table, she announced, "We have a big wedding for *next* spring."

"This whole thing might have been a mistake," he grumbled.

"You've changed your mind about using the vineyard for wedding ceremonies?"

"I'm more concerned about the time you're going to spend working. Do you know how many times those calls have taken you away from Abby and Marianne today?"

Jillian's brow furrowed. "A business is a business, Chase. I'm not organized yet. I'll have to get a private line just for business calls so potential clients can leave messages. Don't forget, I've been doing this since before Abby was born…before Marianne was born," she amended.

"You have to know how much you can take on, but I don't want to see Abby and Marianne unhappy because you're too busy to take care of them."

Eleanor suddenly spoke up. "You know I'll help out."

"That's not the point. No one can replace…a mother."

He could see that fighting spirit flood into Jillian. Taking a deep breath, she looked at his mother. "Could you take the girls into the living room for a bit? Do you mind?"

"I don't mind at all," Eleanor said, getting to her feet. "Abby, Marianne, let's go see if we can find that box of chocolates I hid away for dessert."

Eagerly the girls followed her into the living room.

"You don't have to work, Jillian," Chase insisted immediately, trying to take some of the wind from her sails. "I'll be glad to pay you a stipend so that—"

"Not work? Get real Chase. I intend to remain self-sufficient. You won't pay my way. And I will never, *never* be too busy to take care of Abby and Marianne. You worked after Marianne was born. We're both single parents."

"So you intend to work full-time?"

"I know how to manage my time, and I won't take advantage of your mother. Once we move into the carriage house—"

He interrupted. "We? As in…"

"Me and Abby and Marianne."

"So I suppose they'll live with you half the week and with me the other half of the week? Or with you one week and me the next?"

"I don't want to confuse them."

"Then maybe you should just live in this house."

Her gaze broke from his and she glanced down at her coffee cup. "I don't think that's a good idea."

"I don't think separating them from either of us is a good idea. There's no easy solution here, Jillian. I do think you should be careful about how many jobs you take on right now."

"I thought you wanted the publicity for the winery."

"I wanted you in Pennsylvania. I want you at Willow Creek. If that means you have to plan weddings here, fine. But remember why you're moving here. Remember you're a mother first."

"I don't need *you* to remind me I'm a mother first. I'll always take care of Abby and Marianne the best way I know how."

"You're a strong woman, Jillian, but even *you* have your limits." Frustrated with her and the way the day had developed, he said, "I'm going for a ride. I'll be back in time to help you put the girls to bed."

Grabbing his windbreaker from the peg, he shrugged into it and stepped out into the night air.

Breathing deeply, he tried to exhale all the sensations of having Jillian in the same house, trying to exhale all the complications of a terrifically complicated situation.

Chase's argument with Jillian had unsettled him more than he wanted to admit as he tested wine samples in the lab the next day. As he held one cylinder up to the light, he realized the idea of joint custody tore him apart, even if Jillian was on the same property.

What if she didn't want to live on the vineyard? What if she wanted an apartment or a house?

The idea that she wouldn't stay at Willow Creek gave him an empty feeling that he didn't understand because it had nothing to do with Marianne and Abby.

He was measuring the sugar level of the wine in the cylinder, yet he was remembering Jillian's kisses. He was remembering holding her in his arms. He was remembering how she made him feel when she walked into a room. His logical mind presented an idea he rejected at first, but then he turned it over. There was only one way they could keep the girls together and both parent without losing contact with either of them. Only one way.

If they were married.

When the door of the lab opened, Chase didn't have time to pursue the idea further or to analyze whether it was as crazy as it sounded.

Stan stepped inside the small room.

"Do you want to see the readings on the samples of Whispering Willows?" Chase asked. The wine was a combination of Aurora and Concord grapes. "The sugar level is good."

Crossing to the cylinders, Stan stared down at them, then shook his head. "I don't need to see them. You're the biochemist."

Chase was tired of his uncle's attitude, but he'd always respected him. "Was there something specific you wanted to talk about?" Chase asked, knowing there had to be some reason for Stan coming into the lab.

Turning away from the counter, Stan crossed his arms over his chest. "Eleanor told me Jillian's going to stay in Pennsylvania."

"Yes, she is. It's the only reasonable solution."

"And she's going to live at Willow Creek?"

"We haven't worked out all the details on that yet, but it makes sense for both of us."

"If you're moving her here, that means you intend to stay permanently?"

"Since I've returned, I've realized how much I've missed the vineyard. I think we can win awards again with these wines. Don't you?"

Now Stan looked away, beyond the glass door into

the winery where vats of varying sizes stood. It was as if he was trying to see into the future, or maybe look back into the past. "I'm too old to worry about awards."

"You're only sixty-seven. Some men start second careers at that age," Chase joked.

However, his uncle didn't smile. "I'm not that type of man. I just want—" He stopped abruptly.

"What do you want?"

Stan shrugged and crossed to the door. "It doesn't matter. I'm going to go now. I have a few errands I want to run. I need to buy paint because soon I'm going to start painting the trim on my house."

Stan lived a few miles away near the small community of Columbia. He'd bought an older house and had fixed it up, room by room. It was definitely a bachelor pad and lacked the warmth of a woman's touch. But Stan had always seemed comfortable and happy there.

"Is your crew going to be here tomorrow to bottle wine?" Stan asked.

"Ralph, Jack and Bud will be. If you're here to help, we should be fine."

"I'll be here. I won't start painting the house 'til the weekend."

"If you'd rather not help, I can call Rosa. She said she'd come in any time I need her when her kids are in school."

"I'll be here," Stan snapped, exiting the lab and crossing the wide expanse of the winery.

The sun was setting when Chase returned to the house and he knew he had to smooth the waters with Jillian. She hadn't spoken to him at breakfast this morning and hadn't come to the winery to consult with him on any aspects of the weddings all day. He'd like to spend some time with her, just the two of them and he'd figured out how to do that.

When he entered the kitchen, Jillian was stirring something in a pot on the stove.

"Where are the girls?" he asked.

"Eleanor took them to the attic to search for dress-up clothes. She said she has an old trunk. I think she's just keeping them occupied because she doesn't like them around the stove while I'm cooking."

"What are you making?"

"Chicken à la king. It'll be ready in about fifteen minutes."

Her tone was mildly friendly but more polite than anything else.

"How would you like to go with me into Lancaster tonight? There's a bookstore there I particularly like, and Marianne and Abby could use a few new books."

"I don't know…"

"The store has a bistro with cappuccino. They also have puppets that go with a lot of the books and a music section, too."

"You want input on what you buy the girls?" she asked warily.

"I wouldn't want to go overboard. I figured you'd keep me from doing that."

She almost smiled…almost…and he knew he couldn't snow her and he didn't want to. "I'd like a truce," he added. "Yesterday we both stated our positions strongly and they seemed opposite, but I'm not sure they are."

"You want to talk over cappuccino?"

"Whatever works."

After she studied him for a few moments, she nodded. "All right. I haven't seen much of the area since I've been here. I should start learning my way around."

That evening as they walked into the large bookstore, some of the tension in Jillian from being in close proximity to Chase dissipated. "This looks wonderful."

"I told you it was a good store. It's crowded tonight, though, for a Tuesday."

Most of the patrons seemed to be gathered in the bistro area. As they walked toward the children's bookshelves, Jillian asked, "Did you read much as a child?"

"I was into nonfiction more than fiction, but I did get interested in the *Lord of the Rings* trilogy."

"I read a lot. After my parents were divorced I guess I was lonely and turned to books to escape."

"You didn't see both parents afterward?"

"My father was elusive. He'd make dates with me and break them. Then he moved away and didn't keep in contact. I'd send him letters and they'd come back unopened." Afraid she was telling him too much, she abruptly stopped.

Chase glanced at her as if waiting for more. When it didn't come, he said, "Most of the nonfiction I read had to do with wine-making. I wanted to be an expert at it like my father."

"What happened to change all that?"

He didn't answer as they suddenly confronted a huge sign in the middle of the store aisle:

Tuesday: Five-Minute Date Night
All Singles Meet in the Bistro.


Chase whistled low. "So that's why there's so many people here. What in the heck is a five-minute date night?"

With another look at the sign, Jillian explained, "I've seen this advertised in Florida. Not in a bookstore, though. Usually at some reception center or at a hotel."

"You've been to them?"

"No, but I know women who have. All the men line up and then all the women spend five minutes with each one to see if they want to date them."

The expression on Chase's face made Jillian laugh out loud. "What's the matter?"

"That's a hell of a way to meet people."

She slipped her hands into the pockets of her flannel jacket. "It's hard to meet the right person, and this is one way to attempt it."

Chase glanced over at the bistro and then asked, "Have you dated since your husband died?"

"No, I haven't. How about you?"

His voice was deep and low. "No, I haven't."

She suspected that they hadn't dated for very different reasons. She'd just wanted to concentrate on Abby. Eric had hurt her badly and she'd had no desire to step into that arena again, the arena of men and women's relationships. On Chase's part, however, she guessed the memory of his wife was so strong that he hadn't even wanted to consider being with another woman.

"I hear dating can be fun," she said lightly. "Maybe we're missing something."

"Dating gets complicated," he said with a shake of his head. "Men and women have different expectations."

"Such as?"

"Women want forever, men want a diversion—one night."

"Was that true when you first started dating your wife?"

"We didn't date, not in the way you mean. There wasn't any fanfare or anxiety or the nervousness of getting to know someone new. We worked together so it happened naturally. We started to spend time together, and we just knew we were meant to be together. How did you and your husband meet?"

She didn't want to go back to that night, the hopes she'd had, the butterflies jumping in her stomach because Eric had been so suave and charming to her. "We met at a party, and I did have the butterflies and the nervousness. When we started dating, it was like a dream—flowers, limousine rides, the best restaurants."

An emotion flickered in Chase's eyes but she couldn't read it. It seemed to be akin to sympathy but how could it be when he didn't know anything about her marriage? She wasn't going to tell him, either. Kara had reminded her over and over again she should have left Eric. She shouldn't have let him take advantage of her heart. But Jillian had felt it had been the right thing for her to do—to care for him and to make his last days comfortable. She didn't want Chase judging that or her.

The noise in the bistro section stepped up a few notches.

"I think everyone has a cappuccino buzz already." He pointed to the section of children's books. "At least the kids' corner is quiet. Come on, let's see what we can find."

The children's book section not only had books, there were puppets that accompanied books, additional toys, books that talked, books that lit up.

Jillian selected a Dr. Seuss book that Abby didn't have in her collection. Then she found a Berenstain Bears book that she didn't think Marianne had in hers.

As Chase looked over her shoulder, she paged through the last one she'd picked up. His jaw almost brushed her temple, and the scent of his cologne tantalized her nose. He was wearing a green cable-knit sweater tonight and she knew she'd like nothing better than to be held in his arms. But that was a fantasy moment that could get her in trouble. She realized more than butterflies were jumping in her stomach whenever he was this close. She realized her attraction to him grew stronger each day. She also realized that she was beginning to trust him, at least where the girls were concerned, in a way she never would have trusted Eric.

"You know Marianne already." His deep baritone vibrated through her with an intensity that scared her.

"You're getting to know Abby, too. She was thrilled yesterday when you took her out to ride Prancer. That's one of her favorite things to do now. Soon Marianne will let you put her in the saddle, too."

"Because of Abby."

Their gazes locked and then as if the heat they were generating between them was too steamy for the bookstore, Chase eased back and took a few steps away to look at another shelf.

Although she was aware Chase wasn't far away, Jillian got lost in children's books as she had done when she was a child. She realized she was the one who might go overboard tonight.

She was looking at a red stuffed Clifford who accompanied one of his stories when someone cleared his throat.

She looked up.

There was a good-looking blond man standing there. He appeared to be in his early thirties and was handsome with a square jaw and cleft in his chin. He was wearing a casual blazer and jeans and smiled at her now.

"Yes?" she asked, wondering if he was an employee of the store and she had been doing something wrong.

"I couldn't help but notice you over here looking at children's books. Do you have children?"

Cautious now, Jillian was at a loss for words.

He laughed easily. "I'm sorry. I don't usually ask such personal questions, but I'm here for the date night and I have a son who's five. Are you coming over to the bistro to join in? I'd certainly like to spend my five minutes with you."

A movement behind the man's shoulder caught her attention, then Chase was standing there and she would have given a million dollars to know what was running through his head.

## *Chapter Ten*

Chase found himself standing beside Jillian and taking over. "She's with me," he stated, intimating that meant a hell of a lot more than it did.

His conversation with Jillian about dating had brought home to Chase how hurt she'd been in her marriage. He wished she'd tell him about it. He wished she'd confide in him. But then he hadn't really confided in her either, had he? He'd given her bits and pieces about his background but not the whole story.

When the good-looking preppy had come into the aisle and had eyes only for Jillian, he'd been on alert immediately. Chase had been trying to fight his fascination for her for weeks so he understood how this guy's gaze had locked on her and stayed there. Sensing the man wasn't in the aisle to buy children's books, Chase had paid attention.

Jillian's eyes grew wide but the preppy stood his ground. "Aren't you here for date night?" he asked her, ignoring Chase.

With a look that told Chase she didn't like the way he'd stepped in, she shook her head and gave the man a gentle smile. "No. I just came in… We just came in to buy children's books."

The blond man's gaze dropped to her hand where there was no evidence of rings. "You're engaged?" he asked.

She shook her head. "No, but I'm not interested in date night."

At her response, Jillian's would-be-suitor took a business card from his jacket pocket and handed it to her. "In case you decide you'd like a date, give me a call." Then he winked and headed for the bistro.

Once he'd left, Jillian said to Chase, "I can speak up for myself, you know."

Now feeling disgruntled by the whole episode, not understanding the bite of jealousy he'd never felt before, Chase didn't rise to the argumentative tone in her voice. "I thought I was helping you out. Unless you *want* to go over there to that coffee shop and stand in line. You said you hadn't dated—"

"That doesn't mean I'm not going to date *ever.*" There was still defiance in her voice.

"Do you want to date him?" He motioned to the card in her hand.

Tucking it sedately into her purse, she gave him a small smile. "That's always a possibility."

Chase's jaw clenched. The camaraderie they'd shared for a little while had disappeared. How much *did* he care if she dated another man?

* * *

At the barn the next morning, Ralph Marlowe, who tended to the horses and kept the gardens beautifully landscaped, said to Jillian, "It's early for a ride. The sun's barely come up."

"I saw Chase ride off and I thought it would be a good idea."

They'd left the bookstore last night with a taut atmosphere between them. The drive home had been silent and after they'd put the girls to bed, they hadn't shared conversation or even a "good night." When she'd seen Chase ride off this morning, she'd decided to follow him and clear the air.

"Mr. Chase rides anytime, day or night, winter, summer, rain, shine or snow."

She laughed. "He's a much better rider than I am. Is the trail he takes difficult?"

"No, but he doesn't always stay on the trail, either. I can tell you where he's likely headed, though."

"Sounds good."

Abby and Marianne were still sleeping, and Eleanor had been making sticky buns in the kitchen. This would be a good time to find Chase and clear things up. Though she wasn't exactly sure what she was going to say.

Sure, she'd been angry with him last night at the way he'd handled the man who'd approached her, but then she'd realized perhaps Chase was just being protective. It was hard to know with him sometimes. It was hard to know what he was thinking...or feeling, except where his marriage was concerned. He was always forthright with her about that. He'd loved Fran, and the admiration Jillian had seen in his eyes the night Fran had delivered their baby had been true and sure and real.

Fortunately, Chase stayed on the trail where she'd ridden Giselle before. She'd like to go riding more often but there weren't enough hours in the day to fit everything in that she wanted to fit in. She hadn't even had time to find a computer store that could recommend a tech to check her laptop, which hadn't been reliable lately.

As Jillian rode, she got caught up in the lush, green, new growth of grass; the nearly budding cherry-blossom trees; the blue sky with puffy white clouds piled on top of each other. There were rows and rows of trellises on sloping land with vines coming alive again.

Urging her horse into a canter, she let the wind blow through her hair. Although her hands were cold in the early morning nip, she didn't care as she caught a glimpse of Chase up ahead.

He was looking straight ahead, set on where he was going. That was like Chase. If he was on his way somewhere, nothing could deter him. She'd seen that with the girls and the winery and just in the way he handled his life. He didn't seem to need anyone, and she understood that. She didn't want to need anyone, though sometimes she did need Kara's listening ear, Mrs. Carmichal's arm around her shoulder and definitely Abby's hugs. Marianne's now, too.

When Jillian pulled up beside Chase, he slowed and glanced at her. "You're up early."

"I listened to the Weather Channel last night and it's going to be a beautiful day."

"That's why you came for a ride?"

"One of the reasons."

"And the other?"

Shifting in the saddle, she fingered her reins. "I don't always know how to act around you. Last night when you stepped in, I didn't know why."

Overhead, there was a muted buzz of an airplane. The breeze rustled through pines and maples, cedars and long grass. Everything was coming back to life after the winter cold.

Chase didn't say anything, though, as they continued riding until they climbed to a crest that overlooked the south acreage of the vineyard. There Chase dismounted and held his horse's reins, and she did the same.

While he looked over the winding creek and rows of vines, she studied him. He was wearing jeans and a hooded black sweatshirt. At his neck, she could see he wore a pullover sweater underneath. The breeze whipped his hair back but he faced the wind as if he enjoyed the sensation. She had the feeling Chase was a terrifically sensual man, and she knew she'd tasted only one small element of that sensuality.

"I stepped in last night because I didn't want that guy bothering you. It wasn't until afterward that I realized you might have appreciated the contact."

"It's always flattering for a woman to know a man wants to date her."

Turning slowly, Chase let his gaze wander from her hair to her flannel jacket to her snug-fitting jeans. In spite of the breeze and the early morning chill, she was suddenly a lot warmer.

"Are you going to call him?"

She ran her fingers up and down the length of rein in her hand. "No. I wasn't attracted to him."

Their gazes held and locked, and then Chase's hand was folding over hers on the rein. "You're cold."

His hands were so large, so warm, so full of strength and felt so good covering hers. "Just my hands."

Dropping the reins to the ground, Chase took both of her hands in his and raised them to his face. At first she thought his cheeks were cold to the touch, but then she realized there was an uncompromising heat underneath. His hands over hers on his face were somehow more intimate than kissing. When he tilted his head, his lips were on her palm and she knew what real heat was. The fluttering started deep inside of her as his lips nipped at her palm. A moan escaped from her throat. As his tongue did wonderful things to her lifeline, her knees grew weak.

His gaze didn't leave hers, and she knew he could see what he was doing to her. She shouldn't let him see but she couldn't hide it…just as she couldn't deny the feelings she had for him anymore. She was so attracted to him….

As if her thought translated into his action, he brought her closer, his arms going around her, enveloping her in an embrace that protected her from the cold and her own thoughts and anything that might come between them.

While his lips hovered over hers, he murmured, "You're attracted to me, and I'm attracted to you."

There was no denying it. The way she felt when he held her couldn't be ignored. The way she felt when he strode into a room couldn't be dismissed. The way she felt when he kissed her…

The breeze brushed her hair as his lips sealed to hers. It was a possessive, claiming kiss. Had he been jealous last night? Was that even possible?

His lips and tongue told her it was very possible. His hand lacing in her hair and the tightness of his body told her he wanted much more. Her arms had gone around his neck when he tugged her close. Now her fingers slid into the hair on his neck, and he responded by tonguing her more deeply, by rubbing his lower body against hers, by slipping his hands down her back until they rested on her buttocks. His hands were seductive through her jeans, and she suddenly wanted to touch more of him, too. Her hand slid from his shoulder to his chest.

He broke away with questioning, desire-filled eyes.

"I want to touch you," she whispered, feeling bolder than she'd ever felt before.

"Go right ahead," he growled, and then waited to see what she'd do next.

Her hand flattened on his sweatshirt, and she knew there were layers underneath.

"We're not dressed for this," she said lightly.

"You mean we're not *undressed* for this."

Then he was kissing her again and she was trailing her hand down his chest toward his stomach to his belt buckle. She could feel it under his sweatshirt.

As his tongue mated with hers, as pictures of the two of them together floated in her mind, a desire she'd never felt before overtook her. Her hand continued lower until her palm cupped him, and he groaned.

She knew she was flirting with danger and didn't care. She knew his need was becoming more demanding as was hers. Still she didn't stop.

But he did. His hand covered hers once more, but it wasn't for warmth this time.

"What do you want to happen, Jillian?"

His question hit her with the cold dose of reality that froze her stiff. Didn't she know she couldn't believe in dreams? Didn't she know that although she'd never experienced physical attraction like this, chemistry didn't last? Didn't she know men couldn't be depended on?

She suddenly felt more foolish than she'd ever felt in her life. Pulling her hand away from his, then grabbing the reins to her horse, she took a deep breath. "Obviously I wasn't thinking. I shouldn't have come out here this morning."

"Why did you?"

"I thought we should clear the air."

"Is there something in particular you wanted to say?"

Trying to wrap her pride around her again, she answered quickly. "Yes. I don't need protection from anyone. When a man approaches me, I can handle myself just fine." After those words came tumbling out, she knew she had to be fair. "But I also wanted to thank you. It's been a long time since anyone looked out for me."

"I'm not sure that's what I was doing." Chase's voice was enigmatic, and she knew she'd better not question him because she might not want to hear his answer.

If the atmosphere between them had seemed awkward last night, it was a hundred times more awkward now. "I'd better get back. The girls will be getting up soon."

"I'll ride with you partway. Then I'm going to check on the east slope."

Was he protecting her again? Did he want to make sure she rode back without incident?

After she mounted Giselle, she glanced at him and saw he was studying her. Turning the horse away from him, she headed back to the house.

She'd told him she didn't need his protection...or any-one's protection. Yet she realized she needed protection from herself because she was falling in love with Chase Remmington and didn't know what to do about it.

Chase never knew what to expect when he came home from the winery for supper. Sometimes Jillian was helping his mother in the kitchen, sometimes she was reading to the girls in their bedroom. It was obvi-ous now Abby and Marianne didn't want to be sepa-rated, and Marianne's room belonged to both of them. Some days Jillian took the girls down to the barn in the late afternoon and played hide-and-seek with them among the hay bales.

Actually he was steeling himself to see Jillian again. Every time he thought about her, he thought about her hand on him. That picture seemed to jam up the circuits in his brain. He hadn't wanted to stop her. He'd wanted...

What every man wants—physical satisfaction.

"She's in the living room," Eleanor said. "You won't believe what they're doing."

There was a note of disapproval in her tone.

"What? Playing with Play-Doh on your mahogany coffee table?" He remembered his mother's reaction the first time he and Marianne had done just that.

"No. Marianne saw Jillian painting her nails. She wanted her to paint hers, too. The polish is a light shade of pink, but still...she's only three."

Chase almost laughed out loud but he didn't want to insult his mother. Still he couldn't help but say, "I'll make sure they don't grow up before dinner."

When Eleanor gave him a warning look, he chuckled and headed for the living room.

Marianne was awfully young to start having her nails painted. Maybe he should—

Chase stopped in the doorway when he heard Marianne's laughter. It was light and free and open, and he didn't think he'd ever heard her laugh quite that way before.

The tableau before him was a picture he wanted to store in his memory file for a lifetime. Cross-legged, Jillian and Marianne were sitting on the sofa, facing each other. Abby was kneeling on the floor beside them.

Taking one of Abby's hands, Jillian blew with exaggerated puffs onto her nails. Abby giggled, too.

"Wave them in the air," Jillian suggested. "They're almost dry."

Then she was giving her attention to Marianne again. With extreme concentration, she used the brush on the nail of his little girl's smallest finger. Then she put the top on the polish and set it on the coffee table. Just as she'd done with Abby, she took Marianne's little hand in hers and blew with exaggerated forcefulness on her nails.

Marianne's laughter filled the room.

"It tickles," she managed between giggles.

"No, it doesn't tickle." Jillian playfully brushed Marianne under the chin, and Marianne ducked her head giggling even louder.

"That's what tickles," Jillian said. Then she was tickling Abby under the chin, too.

All of a sudden, Marianne pushed herself up on her knees and encircled Jillian's neck with her arms. "Thank you, Mommy."

Marianne's words immobilized Chase, and he could see they stunned Jillian, too. He realized Marianne was using the word *Mommy* not with the knowledge that Jillian was her mother, but with the heartfelt knowing that she wanted this woman to be her mommy. She knew other kids had moms. She saw them in stores and on TV. She didn't have one and she obviously wanted one.

Moving into the room then, he crossed to the sofa. Jillian's gaze met his and he could see the tears there.

Putting his arm around Abby, he asked, "What are we doing?"

She waved her nails in his face. "Paintin' nails like Mommy's."

He could see that Jillian had a light coating of pink on her fingernails.

"Marianne asked me to paint hers. I didn't think there'd be any harm. I don't think your mother approves, though."

Her voice was a little shaky, and he could understand that.

"Why don't you go show Grandma," he said to Marianne.

"Me, too," Abby chimed in.

"You, too. You know, you might want to think about calling Eleanor 'Grandma' just like Marianne does. I think she'd like that."

At that, Jillian knew Chase had heard Marianne call her Mommy.

Once the girls had run into the kitchen, Jillian swung her legs onto the floor. "She took me by surprise."

"I guess so."

"She sees other kids have mothers," Jillian continued. "It's only natural she wants one, too. Did it bother you?"

"She's *your* daughter."

"Yes, but for three years you didn't know that and now to just change gears… I imagine you always pictured Marianne saying that to your wife."

Jillian's statement should have rung true. After all, he'd thought every day about what Fran was missing, about what Marianne was missing. Yet today, it had seemed so natural for Marianne to look to Jillian as her mother.

"We have to live in the real world, Jillian. The reality is you *are* Marianne's mother."

Silence hung between them for what seemed like a very long time.

Then Jillian stood. "You encouraged Abby to call your mother 'Grandma.' Maybe you should think about asking her to call you 'Daddy.'"

"She will when the time is right."

With insight that had materialized over the past weeks, he realized what he could do to *make* the time right. He realized there was only one solution to this situation with Jillian.

On Saturday afternoon, Jillian and Eleanor were painting Easter eggs with the girls in the kitchen. Tomorrow was Palm Sunday. After church they were going to an Easter egg hunt at a nearby mall.

Jillian was helping Marianne paint a blue stripe around her egg when Chase came in the back door. He was dressed in khakis and a red polo shirt, and he looked so sexy Jillian had to take a breath.

He was smiling as he asked Eleanor, "Can you and the girls finish this project on your own? I'd like to show Jillian something. We'll be about an hour or so."

Although Jillian had no idea what Chase was talking about and she was curious, she still protested. "I can't just leave this mess for your mother to clean up."

"Nonsense," Eleanor said. "If Chase wants to show you something, then it's important. Go ahead."

Jillian looked down at the clothes she'd worn in case splashes and spills occurred. She was wearing a pink T-shirt and her comfortable jeans.

Chase guessed her thoughts. "You're fine. Just grab your jacket."

Jillian had the sudden urge to run a brush through her hair, add some lipstick and make sure everything about her was presentable. Then she chided herself. This wasn't a date.

Still it felt like one as Chase led her out the back door and guided her around the side of the house to the front.

"What's so important I couldn't finish painting Easter eggs?"

"I just picked this up and I want you to try it out before I put it away."

Jillian couldn't imagine what he was talking about. However, as they rounded the corner of the house, she saw it. A black Amish carriage and a huge brown horse stood at the front walk.

"What's this?" she asked.

"Well, if we're planning to do weddings here, I thought it would be a great idea. Not only that, but the girls will enjoy taking rides in it. Want to try it out?"

The idea delighted her and she smiled broadly. "Yes."

Chase helped her into the carriage, holding her hand as she stepped up. His assistance was welcome. As she looked down at him, everything inside of her seemed to come totally alive.

Swallowing hard, she asked, "Where are we going?"

When Chase climbed in beside her, they were close on the wooden seat, shoulder to shoulder, arm to arm. "I'll take the back roads. There's a spot I want to show you."

Flowers were opening now—hyacinths and daffodils. Forsythia was in full bloom. Everything about the day was perfect, vibrant and singing with the beauty only spring could bring. They didn't talk as Chase clicked to the horse every once in a while and glanced at her often.

When she caught him looking, she just smiled and breathed in the warm, grass-filled air, the scent of Chase and the promise of a different life.

She didn't know how long they'd been riding when Chase pointed out a covered bridge. It was obviously old, but refurbished, recently painted, red with white trim.

As they traveled over it, she asked, "Is this safe?"

"Probably safer than a lot of other bridges you go over. Local engineers check it once a year."

They stopped on the other side of the bridge and she turned around to look at it once more. It reminded her of a P. Buckley Moss painting. The artist was an expert at capturing Amish life and bucolic scenes that soothed the heart and soul. Jillian had hung a few framed Moss prints in her town house. Soon she'd pack up all her belongings and she could hang the pictures in the girls' room—and hers—if she stayed in the house.

"Are we still on Remmington property?"

"No, we left it about a quarter of a mile back."

The creek flowed swiftly, foaming over the rocks. It was fast now because of rain that had fallen the past few days. But today there wasn't a cloud in the sky.

"Why did you leave all this?" she asked softly.

"I think it's time to tell you something."

Jillian's heart started beating much faster. "What?"

"Eleanor's not my biological mother."

Nothing could have surprised Jillian more. "You're adopted?"

"No." He wrapped the reins around his palm and stared out at the landscape. "At eighteen, I learned the life I'd led up until then had been a lie."

Although she almost gasped, Jillian withheld comment so Chase would go on.

"I always sensed a distance between my parents, something not quite right. When I went to Scott's house or other friends' houses, their parents were...different than mine. I didn't know how to explain that until I found out the truth.

"How did you find out?"

After a moment, he said, "When I was eighteen, I decided to spend a couple of weeks in Europe with friends. I needed my birth certificate to get a passport. It was in the attic in a safe box. On the certificate I found another woman's name—Doreen Edwards. Rushing to my dad with it, I learned the story. My father had had an affair with Doreen Edwards, who was a singer. She wanted a career and not a baby. When she got pregnant, she was going to have an abortion, but Dad convinced her not to. Eleanor had always had a crush on him, always loved him. Their families had been neighbors since they were kids. Dad knew that and he asked Eleanor to marry him and help raise the child—me."

Her heart ached for the eighteen-year-old boy who must have been devastated. "I can't imagine finding that out, Chase. What did you do?"

"I was so angry with both of them…most of all with Dad. I had put him on a pedestal and he fell off of it that day. All my respect and admiration for him turned to dust. Most of all, I think I felt that way because I knew he'd never loved Eleanor as he'd loved my birth mother. I'm not sure he ever made a real effort to."

"Did you talk about this with him?"

"I was too angry for talking back then. There were a lot of silences the rest of that summer. Then I went to college and I didn't come back except for very short visits. After I got my doctorate, I moved to D.C."

"You were estranged all that time?"

"We were still estranged when Dad died. I regret that now. I feel guilty as hell about it. I suppose I've come to realize that everyone has feet of clay in the right situation. Part of me is still angry that he lied to me all those years, though."

"What about Eleanor?"

"The truth of the matter is, once I got over the hurt, once I realized she'd been backed into a corner, too, by keeping to my dad's wishes not to tell me, I wasn't as angry at her. At first I felt the bonds we'd shared hadn't really existed. But as the years passed, I always thought of her as my mother. I just told her that a few weeks ago, and I think we're okay for the first time in a long while."

"What about your biological mother?"

"I met her. Once. We had nothing in common, and she didn't want a relationship. So that was that."

Jillian clasped his arm. "Chase, I'm so sorry. That's why you told me secrets damaged lives, isn't it?"

"Secrets always come back to bite you. That's why we have to explain to Abby and Marianne as soon as they're old enough to understand what happened."

When she was silent, he asked, "Do you want to get out for a while? I have a blanket."

Something about the way he asked was anticipatory, and she wondered what else he had to tell her.

"Sure. This is a beautiful spot."

Once they were seated on the blanket, looking toward the creek, Jillian couldn't help leaning toward him and clasping his arm. "I'm sorry you had to go through all that. Young adult years are tough enough as it is."

"Yours were tough?"

"At that point, I was still trying to get in touch with my father. I would search on the Internet and get a lead to his address but then I'd write and the letter would come back."

"He didn't come to your wedding?"

It seemed many of Chase's walls had come down as he'd shared his background with her. She could do the same, at least with this.

"I had gotten an address for him and sent him an invitation. But when he didn't even call, let alone show up, I gave up. He might have a new family somewhere and doesn't want his old one interfering."

"I got the impression that that's why my biological mother didn't want to see me. She had her life and didn't want to disrupt it."

Leaning closer to Jillian, Chase cupped her chin in his palm. "*Our* lives have been disrupted by the baby switch."

As his thumb moved slowly over her bottom lip, back and forth and back and forth, she realized he didn't expect a response.

In spite of herself, she'd fallen in love with Chase. The attraction between them had become so much more. She didn't begin to know how she was going to deal with it.

As the breeze carried the scents of spring, Chase kissed her and laid her down on the blanket. She didn't even think about resisting because she wanted this, too. It had been weeks in coming. Chase's kiss was hungry and claiming and so deep and fervent, all she could do was give freely. When he broke the kiss, she wanted more and she knew he could see that in her eyes.

With a deep groan, he kissed her again and pulled her T-shirt from her jeans. His hand slid up underneath it and he tore his lips from hers once more yet kept nibbling, kissing her chin, her neck and her throat. Her hands were on his arms, kneading the taut muscles, wanting to touch more of him, yet totally engrossed in letting him touch her.

As he kissed her temple, sucked on her earlobe sending chills down her spine, his fingers unhooked the front clasp of her bra. Then he was holding her in his palm, running his thumb over her nipple, making her restless and needy and wanton.

When his hand stilled, she wondered what had happened. At the same time, he stopped kissing her.

Opening her eyes, she gazed up at him, feeling the loss of his touch keenly…deep inside.

His brown eyes were dark with his desire for her. But he said, "I'm not going to take this any further until I ask you a very important question."

She waited.

"Will you marry me?"

## Chapter Eleven

Stunned by Chase's marriage proposal, Jillian could only think of one thing to ask. "Why?"

He didn't seem thrown by the question, but then that was Chase. Unless Marianne or Abby were involved, he was fairly stoic. "We have a heartbreaking situation here that can't be settled many ways. Should the girls live with you or me? How and when and where? I think marriage would provide the perfect solution."

"Marriage is rarely a solution," Jillian protested, thinking about Eric.

"Let's face it, Jillian. There's tremendous chemistry between the two of us. Why fight it? Why can't we go into marriage as if it were a business deal that would benefit both of us?"

"A business deal?"

He looked frustrated for a moment and then he

shrugged. "It would be more than that, of course, because we would start sharing our lives. We'd sleep together, eat together, care for the girls together. Those are strong bonds."

Yes, they were strong bonds, she thought. But what about love? What about finding a soul mate? Deep down in her heart, part of her believed Chase could be hers. She'd been afraid to even think about taking that leap. Probably because he wasn't free of his past. Probably because she wasn't free of hers.

She'd thought she'd fallen in love with Eric and what had that gotten her?

It had brought her Abby and now Marianne. She loved both girls, and she loved them dearly. How could she ever be separated from one of them? Or keep them from Chase?

However, marriage was like jumping from a plane without a parachute and she'd still have to trust Chase. Could she do that?

"I need time to think about this."

His voice was low and husky. "I'll give you all the time you need."

He was gazing at her as if he wanted her. However, could she believe he'd be going into this marriage in good faith? Or was he just trying to manipulate her into staying close by so he could be a father to both girls?

She had to be sure before she gave him an answer.

When Chase reached out and brushed her hair away from her temple, he declared, "We'd be good together, Jillian. I think you know that."

The simple sensation of his fingers in her hair made her tremble. Yes, they would be good together—in bed.

But marriage was so much more than that. She still believed marriage should last a lifetime.

On Sunday afternoon, one section of the mall parking lot was covered with straw. As Chase held Marianne's hand, he noticed Jillian was holding Abby's. The girls were enthralled with all the parents and kids, colorful balloons, life-sized rabbits—adults dressed in bunny costumes holding baskets. Each child would receive a basket and when the whistle blew, they would scramble in the straw to find as many plastic eggs as they could. Those eggs would be translated into prizes later, everything from candy bars to stuffed animals. Food vendors and trucks were parked around the periphery of the parking lot selling hot dogs, French fries, ice cream and funnel cakes.

"Can we find eggs?" Marianne asked him, her face filled with the sunshine that gleamed down on everything in sight.

"Not until the whistle blows."

"How many eggs do you think you'll find?" Jillian asked, always ready to teach the girls about numbers.

"A kazillion," Abby answered immediately and they all laughed.

Ever since Chase had driven Jillian home from their excursion in the carriage yesterday, she'd seemed shy with him. This decision was a no-brainer to him. However, he knew asking her to forget what her husband had done to her was a big step. He wished she'd tell him about it. He wished she'd tell him why she was afraid to trust. He knew the black and white of it, but he wanted to see for himself how deeply it had affected her.

After the girls chose the baskets they wanted from a white bunny with a purple jacket, Abby held hers up to Chase. "See? It's pink."

Whenever he looked down into that little face, his heart melted. He still hadn't fully comprehended the fact that Abby was his. When he tucked her into bed at night, he knew he'd never be able to decide between Marianne and Abby. They were both unerringly lodged in his heart now.

Crouching down to Abby, he asked, "You want Mommy to help you find eggs or do you want me to help you?"

"I want *you*," she said and then threw her arms around his neck and kissed his cheek.

Chase took a deep breath and blinked hard, hugging Abby back, wanting Jillian to say "yes" to his proposal more than he'd ever wanted anything in his life.

Marianne was already tugging on Jillian's sleeve and pointing to the kids who were lining up at the starting line. After she whispered something in Jillian's ear, Jillian laughed. She called Jillian "Mommy" now and Chase couldn't wait until Abby began calling him "Daddy."

They lined up with the other parents and children who were four and under. Older kids would have their Easter egg hunt later in the day.

When the whistle blew, they all scrambled for eggs. There was laughter and shouting and giggles and bright-eyed, eager expressions on the children's faces. He and Abby rooted in the straw beside Jillian and Marianne, making their way as quickly as they could yet going slow enough not to miss any plastic eggs.

The smell of the hay was strong, but then suddenly Chase smelled Jillian's perfume as they reached for the same egg.

Children and parents had crowded around them, and someone bumped Jillian. Off balance, she fell into him. He caught her and went down into the hay with her on top of him, his arms holding her tight. At first she was laughing, murmuring something about too many eggs and kids too close together. The next moment she was gazing down into his eyes, and he was looking up at her. The world and the kids and the straw and the eggs all seemed to disappear. His need for her grew so strong he knew she could feel it.

More interested in gathering eggs than what their parents were doing, Marianne and Abby had continued searching through the straw. Chase just wanted to lie there, feeling Jillian's soft body pressing into his hard one, smelling her perfume and her shampoo, caressing her back as if this fall hadn't been an accident.

"We don't want to lose them in this crowd," Jillian murmured.

"No, we don't. And we might get trampled if we don't move soon." His tone was light but he was feeling anything but light.

Jillian seemed relieved, though, as she slid from him and surged to her feet. Then she was locating the girls and he was, too.

After the Easter egg hunt, they stood in line so the girls could receive their prizes. Fortunately, both girls had collected around the same number of eggs. Marianne chose a six-inch bunny while Abby decided on a plastic Big Bird. Afterward, they ate funnel cakes and sat on benches with their drinks, Jillian helping the girls break apart their treats.

Chase watched them, content, as he and Jillian talked about the weddings at the vineyard, passersby and holiday traditions they would like to incorporate into Marianne's and Abby's lives. He knew asking Jillian to marry him had been the right decision.

Now he wanted her answer.

On the drive back to the vineyard, they sang kids' songs, Chase's deep baritone and Jillian's sweet voice melding together beautifully.

After a rousing rendition of "Row, Row, Row Your Boat," Jillian glanced over at him. "I'm surprised you know all these."

"Marianne plays that tape constantly. Some I remember from childhood. I'm not so ancient that I forgot." He was twelve years older than Jillian and he wondered if that made a difference to her. She was mature beyond her twenty-seven years, and when he was around her he never felt more in his prime.

"I didn't mean to suggest you were. Was Fran the same age as you?"

"Yes." He really wished he knew what was running through Jillian's head. The fact that he hadn't let go of Fran's memories? Would that be a determining factor? He couldn't promise her he ever would. Fran was part of his heart, and he couldn't just forget that.

"Does your mother know I know about your family background?"

"I told her last night."

"Good."

Jillian looked relieved, and he realized she didn't

like secrets any more than he did. That was a good thing. They seemed to have like values and that could make their marriage strong. Maybe he was just looking for anything he could use as a bargaining chip. Still, this wasn't about coaxing or persuasion. Jillian had to make this decision all on her own. Once they returned to the house, he was going to take her aside and find out what she had decided. The waiting was driving him crazy.

At Willow Creek an hour later, the girls ran into the house, excited about their prizes, eager to tell Eleanor everything about what they'd seen and done.

As Jillian stepped over the threshold and he followed her, she whispered, "If they tell her about the funnel cakes, she won't be happy we spoiled their supper."

"Probably not," he chuckled. "Hopefully we can delay supper."

When they reached the kitchen, Abby and Marianne were already chattering away to Chase's mother, but Stan was there, too, as well as Ralph. No one looked happy.

"There are shot beetles on the vines," Ralph said quickly. He gave Stan an odd look. "I wanted to start spraying, but Stan—"

Stan avoided Chase's gaze. "I thought we should wait until you got here."

There was something going on here besides beetles on the vines and Chase knew, whatever it was, it would come out in time. He'd been hoping to have that talk with Jillian, but now it would have to wait.

"I'll change and meet you at the supply shed."

Stan started for the back door. "I'll get everything ready."

His mother and Jillian were occupied with the girls so he went toward the front hall and the stairs.

Ralph followed him.

"Is there something else?" Chase asked.

A battered old canvas hat in his hands, Ralph's fingers worked around the rim as if he wasn't sure what he was about to say. "Stan didn't want me to tell you about the shot beetles. At all. I thought you should know."

"I don't understand."

"I don't get it, either. He knows something has to be done. It could be…" Ralph stopped.

"What is it?"

"You know how I respected your father."

"Yes, I do. And he thought highly of you."

"He hired me on when I couldn't read or write and I couldn't get a job anywhere else."

"I know that."

"I owed him, and if you keep me on, I owe *you*."

"You're loyal. I appreciate that." Chase knew patience worked best with Ralph and so he waited.

"Your uncle's not happy that you and Miss Jillian might get hitched."

"How do you know that?"

"I overheard him talking to your mother."

Chase had told his mother he'd asked Jillian to marry him because their decision affected her, too. However, she'd kept her thoughts about it to herself. Maybe she felt more comfortable discussing the possibility with his uncle. "Thanks for letting me know. I'll have a talk with him and maybe we'll get this ironed out."

"Don't tell him I told you."

"I wouldn't do that. Somehow I'll work around to the subject. You did the right thing by telling me."

The older man nodded, then he added, "I don't want to make trouble."

"There won't be trouble. I'm sure Stan had good reasons for not wanting to tell me about the beetles."

He could see Ralph wondered what that reason was and so did he.


Predawn shadows played in Jillian's room as she heard the doorknob on her bedroom door turn the following morning. As it creaked open, she became more awake.

"Jillian?"

It was Chase's voice, and she relaxed. "What is it?" She automatically worried about the girls.

He came into the room then, dressed in jeans and a sweatshirt. "I want to show you something. Grab your robe and slippers."

"But I—"

"Come on, or you'll miss it. I'll wait in the hall."

Having no clue as to what he wanted to show her, she hurried to the bathroom, brushed her teeth, ran a comb through her hair and grabbed her robe. It was pink terry cloth, and she belted it firmly as she slid into her slippers.

Outside her room, he grinned at her and took her hand, looking like a kid with a secret. "We only have about ten minutes."

Letting him guide her, she followed him down the stairs to the kitchen and out the back door. He grabbed his windbreaker on the way out and now he hung it around her shoulders.

After she slid into it, she felt embarrassed because

she probably looked a mess. Mourning doves cooed as she put her hand through Chase's arm and they walked across the backyard and stood between the creek and the winery.

There she saw it. The sky was ablaze with orange and purple and muted pink as the sun just broke through the horizon. She didn't know how long it had been since she'd seen a sunrise.

"It was spectacular yesterday," Chase said. "I thought maybe you'd like to see it today."

The colors rainbowed throughout the sky now, and she knew if she looked away, she'd miss the dawning of a new day. Chase's arm went around her shoulders, and she realized how right it felt there.

She loved this man. Was she deluding herself into thinking they could have a marriage together? Was she deluding herself into thinking he'd ever forget his wife?

When he brought her a little closer, he motioned to the land before them, rows and rows of vines, the sloping earth, the trees along the creek. "In all my travels, I've never seen anything I appreciate more than this."

The signs of spring were all around her—the long green grass, the colorful flowers and the fresh scents of the season. Standing here with Chase felt so real, so absolutely right. She thought of Abby and Marianne and the life they could have as a couple with the girls.

"I thought about your proposal," she said quietly as the sun rose higher and the day began in earnest.

She couldn't tell him she loved him. That love could become a burden he didn't want. It might be an impediment to the relationship they were trying to build. But she knew he had goals and purpose and they looked in the same direction. "I think marriage could give us both what we want."

After a moment, he asked, "What do you want, Jillian?"

"I want a good home for Marianne and Abby. I want to feel safe and secure and know what tomorrow will bring."

Facing her now, he held her chin in his palm. "And do you want to spend your nights with me as well as your days?"

The hunger in his gaze told her he desired her, and she desired him. "Yes."

Chase's kisses had always been seductively sensual. They always coaxed her into passion, hummed through her body and created pictures she couldn't erase. This time when Chase took her into his arms and sealed his lips to hers, there was a different quality about it. There was no coaxing. There was only male hunger and need. It thrilled her and excited her, yet it also made her fear what he might want of her. He wasn't a half-measure man. After Eric's affair she'd wondered what she'd done wrong. If she hadn't given her husband enough…if she hadn't pleased him in bed. Now that old worry came back to haunt her.

She pulled away from Chase, needing to know what he expected before they went any further with this.

His gaze asked why she'd pulled away.

"We're going to say vows Chase. I need to know what that means to you."

Tenderness came into his eyes as well as a gentleness she hadn't seen there before. "Vows mean I'll consider your interests the same way I'll consider my own. Vows mean I'll be faithful to you."

She loved Chase, and God help her, she was beginning to trust him. After Eric died, she'd sworn she'd never trust another man again.

"We don't have to rush into this," Chase told her. "We can plan a fall wedding. And as far as sleeping together, I can wait until you're ready. I want you, Jillian, but I'm not a caveman. I'm not going to force you into anything you don't want."

"Thank you," she murmured, realizing how nervous she'd been about all of it, realizing they still had to get to know each other even more, realizing the girls would have to get used to the idea, too. "I think Marianne and Abby will be happy about this."

After studying her face, he said, "Yes, I think they will be."

"What about your mother? How do you think she's going to feel?"

"We'll find out when we tell her."

Jillian had felt as if she wanted to hug the news to herself for a little while, but they did have to make plans. Chase obviously wanted to put his claim on her and Abby.

He brushed her hair across her brow, and he kissed her again, so deeply she thought they might drop to the ground and make love for the first time right there. His tongue teased her into full-blown desire again. Soon she was pressing into him, feeling his hard arousal.

His hand at her waist, he untied her sash and his hand cupped her breast through her nightgown. When his thumb skimmed over the nipple, he built such a fire inside of her, she was afraid she'd explode.

"I can't wait to touch you all over," he murmured as

her imagination flashed pictures of his big bed, tangled sheets, a night of loving with him. Her cotton nightgown had a button at the neckline and now he opened it. Breaking off the kiss, he trailed several warm kisses down her neck and into the hollow between her breasts. His mouth was so hot on her skin.

When he raised his head, he looked at her and grinned. "I'll give you all the time you need, but that doesn't mean I won't try to convince you we should be in bed together tonight."

She'd seen Chase's playful side now and then and she liked it. Finding her voice, she asked, "Don't you think that might be a little difficult with your mother in the house?"

"We can always go to the barn," he suggested with a grin, buttoning her nightgown again, retying the sash on her robe.

"The barn sounds adventurous."

"Wouldn't that be a good way to start a marriage? With adventure?"

She laughed, and he took her into his arms, holding her close. "This is the right decision, Jillian. You'll see."

She didn't know if he was trying to convince himself or her.

As they walked back to the house, hand in hand, Jillian didn't know when she'd felt this happy. Over the past few years, her work had satisfied her. She'd loved Abby with all her heart and soul. But happiness had seemed to elude her. Today, she felt as if it were almost in her grasp again.

Eleanor was in the kitchen when they returned, mixing biscuits in a large bowl. "You two are out early." Her gaze didn't miss Jillian's nightgown and robe and the jacket thrown over both.

"Chase wanted to show me the sunrise."

"I'm up every morning before dawn, yet I don't think to step outside to see it," Eleanor mused. "I might have to do that tomorrow."

"We have something to tell you," Chase said before Jillian could decide whether to hang up the jacket or keep it on until she reached her room upstairs and could dress.

When Eleanor gazed at them both expectantly, she stopped stirring.

"We're going to get married."

Eleanor didn't say anything for a few moments, then she asked, "When?"

"In the fall," Jillian supplied. "We haven't set a date yet."

"Fall is beautiful at the vineyard." Eleanor returned to her stirring.

"Aren't you going to congratulate us?" Chase asked.

This time Eleanor put down the bowl and the wooden spoon and came over to her son and gave him a hug. Then she hugged Jillian, too. "Congratulations to both of you. I do mean that. I guess we'll have to talk about living arrangements and—"

"Nothing has to change." Chase looked at Jillian and saw she agreed with that. She and Eleanor had come to a peace about living in the same house, but still…

"It might not change for now, but I think as newly-weds, you might want to be alone," Eleanor decided. "I had thought about renovating the carriage house for Jillian, but it might be a good place for me to live."

Jillian was quick to say, "We're not going to put you out of your own house."

"There's plenty of land," Chase protested. "We could

always buy a parcel from you and build our own place. We have time to think about it."

Speaking to Jillian, he gave her a quick kiss. "I have to get over to the winery."

"No breakfast?" Eleanor asked.

"I'll grab a few of those biscuits later."

And he was out the door and Jillian was alone with Eleanor.

"I'd better get dressed," she murmured.

"Jillian, wait."

Steeling herself for what was coming, she wasn't prepared when Eleanor said, "Don't do this because its convenient. Convenient marriages turn into sad ones."

"I know they do," she responded honestly. "I stayed married to my husband because I was pregnant, because I thought the baby should have two parents."

"What happened between you and your husband?"

"Eric had an affair."

"Does Chase know this?"

Jillian shook her head and wondered why she'd told Eleanor when she hadn't told Chase. A moment later, the answer came. For whatever reason, she trusted Eleanor, maybe because she was a woman who'd known heartache of her own.

Eleanor was studying Jillian now and finally she said, "I think we have a lot more in common than I ever suspected."

"My marriage to Chase won't just be for convenience," Jillian assured her. "I have deep feelings for him, and they're growing stronger every day."

Eleanor seemed satisfied with that, went back to the cupboard and took a baking pan from where it was sitting near the canisters. "I think you're good for him. You give him a run for his money. You don't give him everything he wants." Her smile was sly.

"I made too many concessions with Eric. I know better now."

As Eleanor plopped mounds of dough into the pan, she revealed, "Fran wasn't a strong woman, not strong like you are. She always deferred to Chase's wishes. She didn't encourage him to try new things. You do. And the truth is, I didn't see the sizzle and pop between them that the two of you have. They were great friends and that's necessary in a marriage, but it's nice to have more than that, too."

Impulsively, Jillian went to Eleanor and hugged her.

Eleanor asked gruffly, "What's that for?"

"I think I'm going to like having you for a mother-in-law."

"You'd better wait until you're married a couple of years to say that."

The two women smiled at each other, and Jillian felt as if her life were falling into place.

## Chapter Twelve

"I think I'd like the white roses," Jillian said a week later as she chose the flowers she wanted in her own bridal bouquet. She and Chase were consulting with the florist and had selected roses and ivy for the arbor as well as table arrangements in an array of colors for the reception.

Chase said, "See? You really don't need me along for this."

No, she supposed she didn't. But wasn't that what planning a wedding was all about? The couple being partners in that, too? She'd be returning to Daytona on Friday. Would the weekend separation give her better perspective?

She wanted to marry Chase. She loved him. But that was the problem. She loved him, and he didn't love her. He was always respectful of her and hungry for her when they kissed. Would more come? After one marriage where love had turned to betrayal, she should be happy with this partnership of sorts.

The florist was smiling at them. "You've made good choices. Now we just have to select ribbon. I'll go get the samples."

"How can you stand to do this for a living?" Chase asked with a wry smile.

She laughed. "I like choosing the details…just the right touch."

At the word "touch," that deep hunger was back in his eyes and she knew it wouldn't be long until they made love. However, once she did that, there would be no turning back. She would be handing over her heart and soul to him. She had to be absolutely sure before she surrendered her love.

To take the conversation down a different road, she said, "I signed up the girls for nursery school in the fall." The past week had been so busy she hadn't told Chase she'd put that on her to-do list.

The hunger left his eyes. "Why did you do that?"

"Don't you think it's time they broadened their horizons a bit?"

"Horizons? They have each other now. They have Mom and they have us."

Maybe she hadn't told Chase because she'd known she'd meet resistance. "That's exactly my point. They need more. I can teach them numbers and letters and colors, but they need the socialization of other children. Marianne's been so isolated."

"She's been well taken care of," he said curtly.

When Jillian laid her hand on his arm, her voice was

gentle. "I know that. You've done a wonderful job with her. But at some point they start needing more than their parents."

"She'll be scared to death going to a strange atmosphere."

"It's a wonderful school. It's private. I checked everyone's references. For three-year-olds, it's only for two hours, three times a week. It's not as if we're sending them off all day."

"We're not sending them off anywhere. Not yet. Are you doing this because you want more time to work?"

The fact that Chase thought she wanted to foist the girls off on someone else hurt. "No. This has nothing to do with working. It has to do with enriching their lives."

The florist came out of the back room then and came toward the counter, a basket with spools of ribbon on her arm. "Have you chosen a theme color for your bridesmaids?"

A theme color wouldn't be much of an issue. Kara would be flying in to be her maid of honor. Still they should wait until Kara chose a dress to pick flowers for her bouquet. Maybe they should wait on a lot of things.

However, Jillian answered the florist, "I'll get back to you after my maid of honor chooses a dress."

When she glanced at Chase, he wasn't smiling. She couldn't compromise on the things she felt were important. Would he?

After they returned to the vineyard, he was silent and she didn't know if he was freezing her out, or simply thinking about everything.

At the house, they found Eleanor and the girls out

back. Eleanor was transplanting flowers, and Abby and Marianne were playing in a box of dirt.

"What are you girls doing?" Jillian asked crouching down beside them.

"Helping Grandma," Marianne supplied quickly, her focus intent on the mound of dirt she was patting together.

Suddenly Chase was beside Jillian, crouching down, too. "I guess helping is fun."

Both girls nodded vigorously. There were dirt streaks on their cheeks and on their clothes.

Eleanor said, "I put some of Marianne's old clothes on them both so it didn't matter how much dirt they smeared around everywhere."

Abby had a plastic Big Bird in her hand and she was making a hole in the ground for him to sit in.

"How would you girls like to play with some other kids?" Chase asked them.

Abby looked up at him. "I play with kids at play-gwoup."

Jillian wasn't going to say a word. Chase had brought it up, and she was going to let him handle it.

"Do you like playing with other kids?"

Abby nodded.

"Marianne, what do you think about it?"

When Marianne shrugged, the gesture didn't surprise Jillian. The little girl had been sheltered.

Abby told Marianne, "We wead stowies and play with balls."

Marianne tilted her head, looking intrigued. "Will Abby come, too?"

"Yes, Abby would be there, too," Chase answered.

"Okay."

After Chase rose to his feet, he planted his hand under Jillian's elbow and she straightened, too. "Mom, Jillian and I have something to discuss. Are you okay here with them for a little bit longer?"

Eleanor glanced down at her own grimy hands. "We're fine. We have two more trays of plants, and I can always add water to their dirt and let them have some real fun."

As Chase guided Jillian inside, she tingled from having his hand on her arm. His forcefulness sometimes made her hackles rise but other times it simply excited her.

Once inside the kitchen, he raked his hand through his hair. "I'm not used to you yet," he said bluntly.

"What do you mean?"

"First of all, I'm not used to sharing responsibility for Marianne. I've made every decision where she was concerned, as you've done for Abby. It's hard for me to let go of that responsibility."

"It's a shared responsibility now," Jillian reminded him softly.

"I'm beginning to realize that."

"I have to tell you what I think is right."

"I know you do. And I want you to. Just don't always expect me to agree right away."

She smiled and realized she'd done something that was second nature to him. "I should have consulted you about it first. I should have let *you* make some of the phone calls to check references," she added with a smile.

At that, his arms went around her and he caught her to him. "I think I would have delegated that back to you."

She could see that he was teasing, and her heart somersaulted at the look in his eyes. The next moment he was kissing her, and she was forgetting her doubts and looking forward to their wedding.

Chase and Jillian took their time putting the girls to bed that night. After Jillian had kissed Marianne, and Chase had given Abby a hug, she could feel his eyes on her. His kiss had haunted her all day. His kiss had told her exactly what he wanted.

As they left the girls' room, she knew what she wanted, too.

Gently stopping her from going down the hall with a hand on her shoulder, Chase nudged her around to face him. "How would you like to spend some alone time in the barn?"

She couldn't help but tease him. "Alone by myself, or alone with you?"

Catching her to him, he kissed her long and hard and deep. His voice was gravelly when he said, "Definitely alone with me."

His bedroom was only ten feet away as was hers, but in the house, they'd be aware of everything and everyone else, too. "Alone with you sounds good," she said breathlessly.

His low chuckle told her the kiss had had the effect he'd desired.

Downstairs, he ducked his head into the living room where his mother was watching TV. "We're going outside for a while."

Eleanor nodded absently and Jillian was just as glad she hadn't comprehended what they were up to. Sneaking off with Chase could be embarrassing when it came to explanations.

On the way to the barn, his arm circled her waist and the contact made her body hum. The stars were brilliant and there seemed to be thousands of crystals of light. They were like tiny beacons showing her the way to her future. The moon was so full it was easy to see where they were going as they crossed the gravel lane.

She thought they'd go into the lower part of the barn where there were empty stalls. But to her surprise, Chase pulled open the door to the upper level and held it for her as she went inside. Hay bales were stacked in one section and a tractor was parked in another. The smell of night and hay and old wood rode on every breath Jillian inhaled.

"Where are we going?" she asked in a low voice.

"You don't have to whisper," he said with a chuckle. "There are only the horses to hear. Come on. I'll show you."

Taking a ladder from the side of the barn, he propped it against an opening that led to a higher level.

"I've never really noticed this before."

Making sure the ladder was sturdy, he asked, "Think you can make it?"

"Sure. What's up there?"

"The hayloft. I tossed a couple of blankets up this afternoon."

Chase had planned this, and she realized he'd been thinking about making love with her for some time. That made her feel wanted, yet she wished there was more than want.

As she started up the ladder, he stayed below. "Careful," he warned. Each foot rung took her closer to the loft and the intimacy she'd decided to share with Chase.

Once she'd made it to the hayloft, he followed her up the ladder. He'd turned the light on in the barn downstairs and it flowed up through the opening and the floorboards. She couldn't see into the corners and the shadows, and it was still very dark, but Chase solved that problem. Going to the outside wall, he flipped open a lever and a small door opened. Moonlight and starshine shone in. It was such a beautiful night. A lump formed in Jillian's throat.

"If it gets too cold, we'll close it."

The pleasant, seventy-degree temperature of the day was slipping down now. She had the feeling she'd be anything but cold, though.

Chase was wearing a T-shirt and jeans tonight, and as he spread a blanket on the bed of hay, she watched the play of his shoulder muscles and everything inside her quivered. She wanted to touch his shoulders. She wanted to touch him everywhere. And she wanted him touching her.

When he glanced over his shoulder at her, their gazes collided and her mouth went dry.

Lowering himself to the blanket, he patted the spot next to him. "Come here," he urged gently.

As she settled beside him, he put his arm around her and drew her close. Resting his chin on her head, he didn't say anything more as they seemed to breathe in unison.

"I want to tell you about my marriage," she said suddenly. She didn't know where it had come from, but she knew she couldn't make love with Chase until he knew some of the most important truths about her.

Again he was silent and she was almost grateful for

that—feeling faith in him, trusting him as she hadn't trusted a man in a very long time. She began with, "Eric had an affair while I was pregnant."

She felt Chase's body stiffen slightly but she went on. "The signs were there. He'd bought new clothes, had his hair cut a different way, spent more time away from home. At first he claimed it was business and I believed him. But then the hang-up calls started and I found a credit card receipt with his name only on it for flowers and candy and a diamond necklace. I didn't want to believe any of it. I know I was in denial for a while. Even when I found the receipt, I thought—maybe he's going to give me the necklace when the baby's born. But then I found a woman's compact in his car and I laid it all out in front of him. He didn't deny it. He made excuses. He said I looked different pregnant and he'd felt the focus of our lives changed away from us to the baby. Facing fatherhood was a big responsibility and he guessed he was running away from it. I tried to stay calm. I tried to stay rational. I knew shouting and screaming wouldn't help, though that's what I wanted to do. I asked him if he wanted a divorce. To my surprise, he said he didn't. He insisted he loved me."

She looked out into the night and the stars. "I wanted to believe it, but my sense of trust and self-worth got broken along with my heart that day. Still all I could think about was the baby and how Dad had left and what it was like for Mom raising me on her own. So I agreed to stay with Eric and try again."

"Why didn't you tell me this before?" Chase asked gruffly.

"Because I didn't want to seem foolish or weak."

"Staying with him wasn't weak. It was brave."

When she gazed into Chase's eyes, she felt that he meant it. "You do understand," she murmured.

His arm tightened around her and his hand laced in her hair. "I understand you wanted two parents for Abby. But I have a feeling that isn't what you got."

"No, that isn't what I got. He was going out of town a lot. Although I called him when I went into labor, he said he couldn't get out of his meetings. After Abby was born…Marianne," she amended and shook her head. "Babies need so much care and I just put our marriage on hold. Then one day, Abby was six months old and Eric had gone to the doctor's for blood tests because he was feeling tired and bruising easily, and then there it was—the cancer. I couldn't let him go through that alone. We didn't have much left, but he was my husband and he was Abby's father."

"That must have been so hard for you. How long was he sick?"

"Five months. He was in and out of the hospital twice, but then that was it. Hospice Services helped me a lot. I don't know what I would have done without them."

"You're an amazing woman," Chase said, holding her close.

His words were a balm over everything she'd gone through. She'd earned back her self-worth on her own but it was so nice to see a reflection of it in someone else's eyes, hear it in someone else's voice.

When Chase kissed her, it was all gentle seduction. His lips said he understood, his tongue told her he admired her and wanted her, his hands pressing up and down her back molded them closer until she could feel his heartbeat as well as his arousal.

When he broke the kiss, he was breathing rapidly and so was she. "Do you want this as much as I do?"

It was important to him that her desire match his and it did.

"Yes."

That "yes" released all the pent-up wanting between them. As moonlight streamed through the small door, Chase pulled his T-shirt over his head. His hair was tousled, his arms and hands were tanned from being out in the sun. His dark eyes excited her in a way she'd never been excited before. When she reached out to touch him, he sucked in a breath.

As her fingers played in his chest hair, he groaned. "I've waited for this a long time."

She didn't know if he meant with her or with any woman. Chase wasn't the type to have one-night stands.

"I haven't been with anyone since my marriage."

With anybody else, she might think that was just a line. But with Chase, she believed him and that scared her because it showed her how deeply she'd fallen.

With infinite slowness, he undressed her as if he intended each graze of his knuckles against her skin and every touch of his fingertips against the material to be foreplay to prepare her for what they were going to share. She didn't think she needed as much preparation as he thought she did. When she was lying naked on the blanket, he drank in her moonlit shoulders and the starshine in her eyes and she reached for his belt buckle. He let her unfasten the belt. He let her unfasten the snap and zip down his fly.

Then his hands covered hers before she could touch him. "I want to prolong this."

"I just want to feel you inside me."

"You're making this damn hard," he growled.

"Exactly," she said innocently and he laughed out loud. Then his jeans and briefs were in a mound on the hay and he was stretched out on top of her, all hard, long, fit, male. He felt wonderful as she ran her hands down his back onto his backside.

"That's it," he rasped.

But that wasn't it. He wanted to prolong her pleasure and he did that by tonguing her nipple, taking it between his lips, sucking on it. All she could do was raise her knees in silent supplication.

She was surprised when he grabbed for his jeans and used protection. They were going to be married, yet they hadn't talked about more children and he obviously didn't want to stop now to do it. When he pressed inside of her, he did it with need and demand and possession. Everything about Chase's lovemaking thrilled her. Wrapping her legs around him, she moved to the rhythm he set and took him deeper. Her response to his erotic drives took her to a time and place that was strictly theirs. What had brought them together was far away. It was just the two of them, making love in a private place, knowing each other as they'd never known each other before.

Heat building inside of Jillian glistened on her skin. Her fingernails scraped his back as he pressed longer and harder and deeper.

"Now," he decided, rocking against her at just the right tempo...at just the right depth...in just the right place.

The moon burst into a thousand more stars, the heavens rolled and heavenly bodies glistened with rainbow colors as she spiraled into an erotic dimension she'd never known.

Chase's release came moments after hers, and she held him to her as he shuddered. She realized she wanted him to love her the way he'd never loved another woman.

Would she some day be able to tell him that? Would she someday be that honest with him? She was feeling more freedom with him every day and maybe by the time they were married, she could let go of the past entirely and so could he.

She still wanted to tell him she loved him, yet their bonds were new and fragile and she didn't want him to feel he had to say it back. She didn't want to lie there while he couldn't say it back.

When he rolled off of her and lay beside her, his arm went around her. "Are you okay?"

"More than okay," she murmured, her voice catching.

His hand caressed her cheek. "Jillian?"

"Thank you, Chase. I feel like a desirable woman again."

When he smiled, it was teasing and sexy all at the same time. "Give me a few minutes, and I'll show you exactly how desirable you are."

She laughed, threw her arm across his chest and kissed him. Everything was going to be all right. They would parent Marianne and Abby together and, some day, Chase would fall in love with her.

Then she'd have everything she'd ever wanted.

When Jillian arrived in Daytona Beach on Friday afternoon, Kara met her at the airport. Kara was almost as tall as Jillian and slender, with curly blond hair she wore tied back in a ponytail as if she didn't have time to deal with it.

Her blue eyes sparkled now as she hugged her friend and Jillian returned the embrace. "How are you? It seems like years since we've seen each other. I can't believe you're going to get married in a few months. Are you sure about all this?"

Kara was always bluntly sincere and Jillian liked that about her. But right now, she wasn't sure she wanted to deal with it.

The past few days with Chase had been wonderful, but she'd left Willow Creek, her emotions in a turmoil. The girls had seemed oblivious to her leaving. They were like sisters now and loved being with Chase and Eleanor as well as with Jillian. Eleanor had loaned her her car for the drive to the airport. Although Chase had kissed her goodbye before she'd left, she thought she'd felt a guardedness in that kiss. She was afraid again, afraid that the marriage Chase proposed had more to do with the girls than with her. Would he ever truly love her?

Leaning away from Kara, she smiled. "I thought I answered all your questions in our e-mails."

"Not the important ones. Are you having second thoughts about marrying Chase?"

"Kara."

"I know, I know. Give you time to breathe. If I do that and you get caught up in the party, we'll never talk. I know you, Jillian Kendall."

Jillian pulled up the handle on her small overnight case. "So you say."

"You've told me what he looks like, and he sounds like a hunk. But I want the inside info you won't send me in e-mail. Have you slept with him yet?"

"You're hopeless," Jillian protested.

"Nope, just determined. I'll get every last detail out of you, you just wait and see."

But Kara didn't get every last detail out of Jillian as they drove to her town house and made sure everything was ready for the party the next day. Jillian was reticent to talk about Chase and she concentrated on telling Kara about her days with the girls instead.

They were going over lists for the senator's party when Kara said, "Mrs. Grayson was so afraid you wouldn't be here."

"I'm sure they trust you to handle everything."

Kara shook her head. "Not in the same way they trust you. She was in a tizzy when I told her we had to substitute the mocha cheesecake for the double fudge. You can handle her so much better than I can."

Senator Grayson's wife tended to worry needlessly and Jillian could usually use logic to calm her down. "I should give her a call and assure her we have everything under control."

"That would probably be a good idea."

As Jillian stood to use the phone, her doorbell rang. She answered it and found Loretta there. "Hi, there," she said with a big grin. "I was going to stop over and see you in the morning."

"I thought you might be too busy with the senator's party and all."

"Never too busy for you," Jillian assured her. "Come on in. Kara's here."

"Are you two working? If you are, I wouldn't want to bother you."

Kara stood and shuffled her many lists into a folder, then thrust it into a leather carrying case. "I've got to shove off."

"Hot date tonight?" Jillian teased.

"No, just a date. I met him last week at that chamber of commerce dinner. We're having coffee. That's all."

After Kara gathered her things, she gave Jillian another hug and whispered in her ear, "You didn't tell me everything and I know it. We'll talk again before you leave."

Jillian had filled Kara in on some of the things she'd done with Marianne and Abby and how she did feel like a mother to both girls. She'd also explained how she felt closer to Eleanor. But where Chase was concerned, she'd kept silent.

After Kara had left, Jillian said to Loretta, "Come in to the kitchen and I'll make you a cup of tea. I've missed you."

"And I've missed you and Abby. But I suppose that's going to be the way it is now. You're going to move up there to Pennsylvania, aren't you?"

There was real sadness in Loretta's voice and Jillian felt as if she were leaving a favorite aunt behind.

"Yes, I'm going to move to Pennsylvania and there's something else to tell you, too. I'm going to get married."

Loretta Carmichael's eyes grew large and her mouth rounded. "Oh, my goodness. Just who are you going to marry?"

"I'm going to marry Abby's father, Chase Remmington."

"Are you sure about this, Jillian? Are you doing it so you don't have to leave either of the girls?"

"It's much more complicated than that. Chase and I have become close. He's a great father."

"And how does he feel about you?"

Turning away from her friend, Jillian filled the teapot with water and set it on the stove. Without answering that specific question, she said, "He's been so good to us. You'd love the vineyard. Maybe you could take a trip up. Abby would love to see you."

Loretta fidgeted with the collar of her hot pink and turquoise flowered blouse. With worry in her eyes, she went to the cupboard and plucked out two mugs. After some hesitation, she asked, "Did you know Mr. Remmington called me?"

Everything in Jillian went perfectly still. "When?"

Carrying the two mugs to the table, Loretta sat on one of the oak chairs. "Back in February. I remember I talked to him in the afternoon and then you called me that night to tell me the surgery had gone well with Marianne."

"You didn't tell me he'd called you."

Loretta popped up from her chair again, went to another cupboard, and pulled out a box of peach tea. "No, I didn't tell you. I was afraid I'd told him too much and you'd be upset with me. He just had this way of making it easy to talk…."

Although Jillian's heart was racing, she told herself to stay calm. "What did he want?"

"I probably shouldn't have said anything," Loretta mumbled, taking the tea bags to the table.

"Loretta, you know you can tell me anything. I won't be upset with you."

"I know you don't like to discuss your private life, but he was asking me if you were a good mother and all. Of course, I told him you were. And then somehow, we got into Eric and I told him Eric had treated you badly, that he hadn't been faithful, but you were loyal to him to the end. All good things. I thought that was important and he seemed to be concerned about you being with his daughter."

Chase was concerned with her being with Marianne? Couldn't he tell from the way she'd cared for Abby that the girls would come first, foremost and always? Why hadn't Chase told her he'd called Loretta? He'd acted as if he hadn't known anything about Eric. What was going on?

Seeing that Loretta was looking upset, Jillian went to her and put her arm around her. "It's okay. No harm done. You were just telling the truth."

"And he didn't tell you that he called me?"

"No, he didn't."

As soon as Jillian returned home, she was going to find out why.

## *Chapter Thirteen*

In front of his computer, Chase studied the job offer from the Food and Drug Administration for a second time. A year ago, he might have considered it and moved to Arkansas for a position doing research in his field and a competitive salary. Now, however, Arkansas just wasn't where he wanted to be. It wasn't the vineyard. He wouldn't even think about uprooting Marianne again. Besides, Jillian and Abby were starting to love Willow Creek as much as he did.

He missed Jillian.

On Friday, his mother had offered Jillian her car to drive to the airport and then return on her own. Independent woman that she was, Jillian had liked the idea.

Chase had to smile. Damn independent.

However, the smile faded when he considered how quiet Jillian had been since her return this afternoon and throughout dinner. Her reunion with the girls had been ecstatic. Afterward, though, something troubled him about her demeanor. When he'd taken her in his arms to kiss her, she'd pulled away. Something was going on in that head of hers and he needed to find out what it was. Maybe her party had been such a success she was worrying about starting all over here.

He couldn't believe how much he'd missed her while she was gone. He couldn't believe his happiness was tied up with hers so intricately.

He was about to shut down the computer when he heard a vehicle on the gravel outside. He knew the sound of Stan's truck. It had a particular growl that he always recognized.

A few minutes later, his uncle came through the tasting room, then entered Chase's office. Chase was still puzzled about things Ralph had told him concerning Stan. He just hadn't figured out the best way to approach his uncle.

"I didn't expect to see you back here tonight," Chase said.

"I remembered something I wanted to enter into the computer. If I wait until tomorrow, I might forget where I put the receipts." Stan laughed but Chase didn't see a real mirth in his eyes. His uncle looked uneasy.

Standing, Chase turned the swivel chair toward Stan. "It's all yours. I'm going to put the girls to bed."

"Is Jillian back?"

"Yes, she got in this afternoon."

"I guess you two will have a reunion of sorts tonight." Stan's smile was sly.

All day, all weekend, Chase had looked forward to tonight.

"I'm just hoping Jillian has realized her decision to stay and marry me is the right one," Chase said honestly.

"I don't see why she wouldn't want to stay. Willow Creek is one of the most perfect spots on this planet, and I've seen a few."

His uncle had seen a tour of duty in the service and had traveled then.

"Yes, it is," Chase agreed. "It's going to be a wonderful place to raise children."

"Jillian still might not want to share a house with Eleanor, though. That new development going up over on White Rock Road could be just the place for you."

Chase had seen the elegant houses under construction there, but that wouldn't be the same as living on the vineyard. "I spoke to Mother about possibly buying a piece of property here. We could build a house and be within shouting distance."

"I suppose that's an option," Stan mumbled, sitting down at the computer.

"I think there's apple pie in the kitchen," Chase offered, hoping Stan would come over to the house and they could have a meaningful conversation.

Stan patted his waistline, which was thicker than it used to be. "Nah. The doc says I have to watch what I eat."

Chase had never known his uncle to count calories or watch his cholesterol, but maybe he was turning over a new leaf. Stan was preoccupied now. Chase would ask his mother to invite him to dinner on Sunday. Then perhaps his uncle would confide what was bothering him.

A few minutes later, Chase was letting himself into the house. His mother was making herself a cup of tea.

"Jillian's giving them a bath. Did you hear them squealing the whole way over to the winery?"

Marianne and Abby loved to splash in the bathtub. "No, but I hear them now. I'll go up and see if I can get wet, too."

When he reached the bathroom, he found the girls pouring water over each other's heads with tiny pastel colored tugboats.

He grinned as he stepped into the bathroom. "It doesn't sound like anyone's having fun in here."

Marianne rattled off a string of everything she'd been doing since supper. She was talking so much more now since Abby had arrived.

Jillian was sitting on the side of the tub holding a towel. "Come on, you two. You're going to shrivel up if you stay in there much longer. Whoever can dress in their pj's the fastest can choose the book we read tonight."

Jillian was good at making up games so the girls could learn or be coaxed without an argument. Now they each wanted to scramble out of the tub first.

He took a fluffy green towel and held it out to Marianne. "Need some help?"

"We can always use help," Jillian said but kept her gaze averted. He was going to find out what was troubling her as soon as the girls were settled.

While Buff also listened intently to the story with Abby and Marianne, Chase read to them from a Raggedy Ann book. After he gave them giant hugs and sloppy kisses, after Jillian had whispered a last goodnight, they stepped out into the hall.

When Jillian would have gone toward the stairs, Chase caught her arm. "Let's go to my room."

"I don't think that's a good idea. I'd like some privacy because we need to talk. But your bedroom—"

"Are you afraid of me, Jillian?"

She looked startled. "No."

"Do you think I understand the meaning of the word 'no'?"

At that, her gaze finally met his as she caught his meaning. Her cheeks flushed. "I suppose you do."

Closing the gap between them, he lifted her chin. "There's no supposing about it. If you want to talk, we'll talk. I have a sofa in there as well as a bed."

She looked at his closed bedroom door. "All right," she acquiesced softly.

As he entered the room, he switched on the dresser light but the soft yellow glow didn't reach the sofa on the other side of the room. His furniture was a heavy dark pine. The drapes and bed cover were patterned in wine and navy. He didn't think Jillian had ever been in his bedroom. Now she followed him to the long sofa, and he lit the small table lamp in that area, too. She was wearing pale yellow sweatpants tonight and a white T-shirt. He caught the scent of spring and flowers and Jillian. She must have showered and changed after supper before she gave the girls a bath.

"What happened in Florida?" he asked wanting to get to the root of the problem right away. "Did the party go well?"

They hadn't really talked about Senator Grayson's daughter's party. The girls had been chattering through dinner about everything they'd done while Jillian was away.

"The party went very well. Senator Grayson wanted me to plan a fund-raiser for him."

Chase tensed. "Are you going to?"

"It would be a little difficult if I'm living here. Kara's going to do it. I told him he'd be pleased with her."

She squared her shoulders a bit and raised her chin, signaling to Chase that the party wasn't what she wanted to talk about. "I want to know why you called Loretta Carmichael."

So Loretta had talked to Jillian about his call. That wasn't totally unexpected. "I called her to find out if I could trust you with Marianne."

"I see. Were you afraid I'd run off with her?"

"I didn't know what you'd do, Jillian. You were a stranger. My P.I. had given me a basic report on you, but that wasn't enough. If you were going to be spending time with my daughter, I needed to know more." He realized he still thought of Marianne as his daughter no matter what the DNA test had said, and he felt just as connected to Abby now, too.

"You knew about Eric before I told you," she accused him.

He shifted closer to her, stretching his arm along the back of the sofa. "Yes, I did. Loretta filled me in, and I was glad she did. It explained a lot, especially why you wouldn't talk about your marriage."

"Why didn't you tell me you knew?"

He looked straight into her eyes and told her the truth. "Because I wanted you to trust me enough to confide in me, especially after I learned about your husband's affair. I knew how painful that had been for you and I didn't want to force the information from you. I wanted you to tell me freely."

Her gaze lingered on his face as she seemed to sift every one of his words for their true meaning. Finally, she nodded. "That makes sense."

"Why did *you* think I had called Loretta?"

"To gain ammunition for a custody battle."

"I wouldn't have found any. You're a good mother. You were a loyal wife."

Tears rose up in Jillian's eyes, and Chase wondered if trust was always going to be an issue between them. How could they have a good marriage if it was? He and Fran had trusted each other so completely.

Drawing Jillian into his arms, Chase tucked her into his shoulder. "I know you're going to miss Loretta."

Jillian tipped her face up to his. "I'm going to miss her, but I'm ready to start a life here with you."

He'd been waiting for those words. He'd been counting on them. His lips found hers hungrily. He'd missed her. He'd missed her more than he'd ever imagined he would.

When Jillian didn't hold back, when her tongue stroked his, when her fingers laced in his hair, he took her onto his lap and began to undress her. She tugged his T-shirt from his jeans.

After he slid her sweatpants down her hips, she kicked them off. Their getting naked took hardly any time at all. He had to have her now. Only he wanted to show her that trust wasn't about *his* satisfaction. It wasn't about only this moment. It wasn't about desire that might fade thirty years from now.

When she was naked on the sofa, he caressed her breasts, kissed her nipples, ran his hands down her thighs until she was restless and wanting and needy.

"Chase," she pleaded.

"You're going to like this," he growled. The effort of keeping a lid on his own restraint was costing him.

She opened her eyes, and her gaze met his. "I always like when you touch me."

"I'm going to do more than touch you." Then he moved down her body and spread her legs apart.

When he ducked his head to her navel, she gasped. When he moved even lower, she almost sat up. "Chase."

Lifting his head again, he smiled. "Relax, Jillian. Just enjoy it."

Her eyes were questioning, and he realized she'd never been loved in just this way before. That thought aroused him even more.

He wanted Jillian to trust him even in this…especially in this. His fingers played in the brown curling hair at the vee of her thighs. She moved against his hand. Stroking her more intimately, he noticed her cheeks becoming flushed, her breathing becoming more shallow.

"Give yourself up to it, Jillian. Let yourself go."

Between his gentle urgings, he kissed the inside of her thighs and came closer and closer to her center. When her restlessness increased, she grabbed at the sofa cushion and he knew it was time.

With his tongue, he touched her at the most intimate place a man could touch a woman. He teased and taunted until she was whispering his name. Circling the tiny nub with his tongue, his lips enclosed it, and Jillian cried out. Her orgasm seemed to go on and on and on and Chase took great pride in that. He saw the wonder on her face, the prolonged satisfaction her body was expressing. As her climax subsided and he watched every part of her body relax, she floated back to earth.

"Let's see if we can make it happen again," he murmured, rising above her, entering her with measured restraint.

After a few moments, he started moving inside her, slowly at first, utilizing every bit of his self-control. But then self-control became a concept that no longer applied. He was thrusting deeply, her fingers were kneading his shoulders, and he was losing himself in their passion as completely as she had.

She whispered against his neck, "It's happening again."

He took them both to the peak of anticipation, the peak of erotic pleasure, and when he heard a second cry of release from Jillian, he tumbled over the mountain with her. Nothing had ever felt so absolutely right. He realized that even if Abby and Marianne weren't in the picture, he'd want Jillian in his life.

They slept together that night, all night, and Chase didn't care if they had to make explanations to his mother. So be it. They were engaged.

Engaged. He had to buy Jillian a ring. Tonight. He'd do it tonight.

It was still before dawn when he left the bed, still thinking about how they'd made love most of the night. After a quick shower, he dressed, gave Jillian a soft kiss on her temple that didn't awaken her and went straight to the winery.

At first, when Chase stepped into the building, it seemed shadowy, cavernous and empty. But then he heard the scrape of metal on concrete.

A sixth sense kept him from shouting out. He strode

to where he'd heard the sound and then he froze. Stan was on a ladder, reaching toward the top opening of the vat. In his hand was a beaker.

"What are you doing?" Chase demanded, already afraid that he knew.

Stan was stonily silent until he reached for the opening again and Chase was up the ladder, grabbing the beaker, and wrenching it from his uncle's hand.

A look at it, a whiff of it, told him it was vinegar bacteria and it would ruin the wine.

At that moment, he wanted to throttle his uncle. He wanted to shake him and demand to know why he would ruin any part of what they'd worked so hard to bring to fruition.

Instead he climbed down from the ladder with the beaker and said tightly, "If you don't want me to call the police, tell me what you were doing."

After Stan descended the ladder, his face was belligerent.

Restraining his anger, Chase went to the small lab and tossed the contents of the beaker down the sink. Then he ran the water to give himself more time to cool down.

Stan had trailed him inside.

"What in the hell were you thinking?" Chase finally asked, facing his uncle.

When Stan didn't respond, a moment of clarity suddenly fell into place. "You've been trying to sabotage the vineyard since mother asked for your help," Chase realized. "It wasn't an accident that wine didn't reach clients on time, that shipments landed in the wrong place, that ads weren't mailed by the deadlines. I cut you some slack because I thought you were just upset over losing your brother."

"He was your *father*, too," Stan snapped.

Chase waited.

Stan's face reddened as he jammed his hands in his overall pockets. "You acted as if he hadn't given you *everything*. You acted like you were perfect and because he'd made one mistake, you didn't want him in your life anymore. Do you know how much that hurt him?"

Chase knew he had a lot to answer for where his father was concerned and the regret haunted him. But he wanted Stan to understand something, too. "Do you realize he lied to me for eighteen years? Do you understand that I lost my mother that day, that our relationship changed?"

"Eleanor *is* your mother," Stan said stubbornly.

"I know she is and I told her that. And I have regrets about that, too. I wish I'd have come home and we would have worked everything out sooner. But it didn't happen. That doesn't explain why you're trying to sabotage the vineyard."

Stan seemed to age before Chase's eyes. His shoulders slumped and he leaned against the counter. "I love your mother. I always have. But she only had eyes for Preston. He didn't deserve her. He never really loved her. After he died, I was hoping she'd sell this place, and she and I could have a life together. Instead, she called *you!*"

Chase was absolutely stunned. He'd known Stan and his mother were friends all these years, but he'd never suspected anything else. Then, of course, he hadn't been around and when he'd returned, his attention had soon focused on Marianne.

"So you thought if you could cause some trouble, my mother would sell the vineyard and go off with you somewhere?"

"I knew it wouldn't be that easy. But I thought once she sold the vineyard, we'd have time together. She'd see that I was more right for her than Preston had ever been."

His anger gone now, Chase pitied his uncle. "Have you ever told Mother how you feel?"

Looking sheepish and a bit embarrassed, Stan shook his head.

"I think you'd better. It's hard to love a ghost, and I think Mother's been letting go of Dad more than you know."

After a stretch of silence, Stan mumbled, "Are you going to call the cops?"

"Have you ruined any other vats of wine or is this your first try?" Chase asked wryly.

"I haven't touched anything else. I was hoping you'd get disgusted with the whole process and leave."

"What do you want, Uncle Stan?"

The title seemed to get to his uncle and he ran his hand over his face. "I'm tired of being a hired hand, a second mate. Maybe I should just stop working here."

"What else would you do? Go fishing?" Chase knew his uncle needed to be busy, and he thought he had a solution. "How would you like to invest some money in the vineyard and become a partner?"

"You'd let me do that?"

"If you're serious. If you want to make Willow Creek Estates wine the absolute best in the country as I do."

"If I had a vested interest in the winery, I'd feel like working here meant something, like I was doing something Eleanor could be proud of."

"All right. You decide how much you want to invest. I'll have my lawyer draw up the papers."

"I can't believe you're doing this. Not after what I tried to do."

"I never realized how you felt about my mother. Now that I look back, it's obvious."

"Are you going to tell her?"

"I think you should tell her, don't you?"

Stan sighed. "I suppose so, but it'll take me a little while to work up some courage. Give me some time."

"I'll give you until the partnership papers are drawn up. Mother will have to okay it."

Stan nodded. "Thanks, Chase. Preston raised a good son. I'm sorry I've been giving you such a hard time."

"That's going to change now. A lot of things are going to change."

Chase didn't know what the future would bring for Stan and his mother, but he hoped it was happiness— the kind of happiness he was going to find with Jillian.

When Jillian came into the kitchen with her laptop computer, she felt as if she were sitting at the end of the rainbow and had just discovered the pot of gold. Last night with Chase had been wonderful and she couldn't wait for many, many more nights like that.

"Good morning," Eleanor said as Jillian entered the kitchen. "Sleep well?"

There was something in Eleanor's tone that made Jillian think the older woman knew she'd spent the night in Chase's room. Feeling her cheeks flush, she busied herself with setting the laptop on the table.

"Fine," she answered calmly. "And you?"

"Just fine. Do you think the girls will want pancakes this morning?"

"Probably. Do you want me to help? I can do this later."

"No, I can handle this. What are you doing?"

"Estimate sheets for this new wedding we picked up." However, when Jillian opened the case and pressed the switch to start the computer, it wouldn't boot up. She'd brought the charger along, too. Going over to the counter, she plugged it into the outlet but still the computer didn't boot.

"Problems?"

"This has been giving me trouble. I wanted to replace it, but with everything that's happened, I just didn't have the time."

"You could use the computer in Chase's office."

Jillian considered that. "I do have everything backed up and he must have some sort of word processing program on his computer."

"Sure he does. I've written articles on his computer already."

"What kind of articles?"

"For wine-tasting magazines…for the area wine growers' newsletter."

In some ways, Eleanor was as multifaceted as her son and Jillian enjoyed getting to know her. "I'd like to read them some time."

"I have copies upstairs," Eleanor said a bit shyly. "I keep a portfolio."

Closing up the laptop, Jillian set it in an out of the way place on the counter. "I'm going to go over to the office. I have about an hour until the girls get up."

"If you run into Chase," Eleanor said with a straight face, "tell him I hope he slept well, too."

Jillian felt herself blush and then she smiled. "I'll do that."

Five minutes later, she opened the door into the winery, wondering if Chase was there. She didn't see or hear any movement. He could be anywhere, checking the vines, talking to his staff. Crossing the tasting room, she opened the door into Chase's office. Finding the button on the computer tower, she turned on the machine and the monitor, too. His computer booted up in seconds. Fortunately, she saw Chase used the same word processing program she did.

Sitting in front of the machine, she remembered she'd told Kara she would e-mail her this morning. Kara just wanted to know she'd arrived at Willow Creek safely.

This morning Jillian felt a lot more than safe! Her smile grew wider.

Clicking on the icon for Chase's e-mail program, the screen displayed his in-box with the last message he'd received open on the bottom half of the screen. Her eyes widened at the subject heading—*Job Offer.*

She shouldn't read it. She *knew* she shouldn't read it. Yet she couldn't help but read it. The job offer had come from a contact of Chase's at the Food and Drug Administration. Along with salary, it offered expenses for Chase to move to Arkansas.

Arkansas.

Why hadn't Chase mentioned this?

Was he keeping it from her?

The girls loved Willow Creek and so did she.

Then all Jillian's doubts came flooding back. Chase was still Marianne's legal guardian. He was Abby's father, and now he had proof of that. If he wanted to leave and cut Jillian out of the picture...

She had to find out now. She had to find out what he was planning. She had to know if last night was a true meeting of hearts and souls, or if Chase was just using her until he made a new life with the girls...*without* her.

## Chapter Fourteen

When Jillian emerged from the wine-tasting room, she scanned the grounds as far as she could see for any sign of color. Almost out of sight, along the trellises bearing Aurora grapes, she saw two figures. The taller man was Chase.

Her heart both soared and sank. Had last night been simply a dream? Had she deluded herself about Chase as she had with Eric? If his wife still filled his heart, how could he make room for her?

Taking off at a run, she hardly noticed the creek running fast and furious, pushing at its banks. As she covered the distance between them, she sank into mud from the spring rain. Closing the gap between her and Chase, she saw he was talking to Stan. His uncle was pointing north toward the crest of a hill.

So deep in their discussion, Chase didn't see her

until she was practically upon them. His smile turned to a worried frown. "Is something wrong?"

"I need to talk to you."

Stan looked from one to the other and said to Chase, "And I need to talk to your mother."

As Stan left, Chase curved his arm around Jillian's shoulders. "What's so important?"

Pulling away, she gazed up at him, searching his face. "My computer crashed and Eleanor said I could use yours. I opened your e-mail program to send Kara a message that I arrived safely and—"

Chase's expression changed. It closed and became somber. "And?" he repeated.

"And... Why didn't you tell me about the job offer from the Food and Drug Administration?"

"You were in Florida when it came in."

"I've been back since yesterday afternoon. Are you going to take it?"

Where his expression had been serious before, now it turned angry. He was dressed in a green T-shirt and tight-fitting jeans, and he had never looked more powerful or masculine or confident. "I thought after last night you finally trusted me."

"Trust goes two ways," she returned defensively. "You called Loretta and you didn't tell me."

"That was when I hardly knew you. I explained last night why I didn't tell you I'd talked with her."

"Because you wanted me to confide in you on my own. That's a convenient excuse, Chase. We could have gotten it all out in the open—"

"You wouldn't talk about your marriage."

"I *told* you about my marriage. You know everything

about me now. So why didn't you tell me about the job offer?"

"I didn't tell you because I'm not considering it. What did you think I was going to do? Break our engagement? Take the girls to Arkansas and leave you here?"

When she didn't respond, he muttered, "My God. That's what you thought. Jillian, are you ever going to trust anyone again? Don't you realize I'd never do anything to hurt Marianne or Abby and that includes taking them away from you? If you believe I would do that, we shouldn't even consider marriage. If you can't trust me, we'll never be more than co-parents."

Jillian felt devastated, mortified and ashamed. "Chase, I'm sorry. I was afraid—"

"*I'm sorry* doesn't cut it. And being afraid that I'm going to turn around and betray you at any time will ruin a marriage. We'd better rethink our plans before we make a mistake we can't rectify."

Then Chase was walking away from her, furious at her, leaving her standing alone in the vineyard he loved.

On Monday, Jillian put the to-do list for Sherry and Tom's wedding aside, unable to concentrate on anything. It had been two days since her argument with Chase, two days since she'd accused him of betraying her, two days since she'd realized trust could be a choice as well as a feeling. She'd let her marriage to Eric color her entire world and now her inability to get beyond it had possibly destroyed her future with Chase.

He hadn't come near her since that morning, not unless the girls were around. Even then, his eyes held no warmth, and his lips no smile. She knew an apology would never be enough but she couldn't figure out what to do or say. She wanted to be his wife.

On the other hand, part of her was wondering if he closed himself off because he wasn't ready to go on, either. Maybe he wasn't ready to leave the memories of Fran behind and form lasting bonds with her.

Eleanor had taken the girls outside for a walk so she could work. She couldn't work. She might as well find them and enjoy their company while she figured out a way to ask Chase to forgive her.

As she walked out the back door, the screen door banged behind her. Looking to the west then the east, she spotted Eleanor and the girls and Buff walking through the grass between the winery and the creek. Rain yesterday had made everything even greener. The trees, the grass and the flowers were bursting with new life.

The unevenness of the ground didn't stop Buff from playfully darting in and out of the peony bushes along the winery. It didn't stop Marianne and Abby from chasing him and then falling behind when Eleanor called them to her.

The day's temperature could hit eighty, and as Jillian walked toward the winery, her gaze on Marianne and Abby, she realized she'd soon have to buy summer clothes or ship everything from her town house to here. No matter what happened with Chase, she was staying. She loved him. Maybe some day he would believe that.

Her thoughts on Chase, she was barely aware of Buff scampering away from the girls. Then her attention was drawn to him as she realized he was chasing a squirrel.

She could see Eleanor catch Marianne's hand, but she wasn't quick enough to catch Abby's. Abby zoomed off after Buff, determined to catch up.

In the next few moments, panic turned to fear and then horror as Buff headed for the creek after the squirrel. Taking off at a run, Jillian saw Buff scamper down the bank, Abby close behind him.

Then Jillian's heart stopped as Abby slipped on the muddy bank and toppled into the creek. Swift water rushed past her and swept her away.

Jillian didn't think. She ran even faster to the edge of the bank, stumbled down through the mud and jumped into the water. Buff was scrambling up the muddy bank and finally found footholds in some laurel.

Abby's terrified cries wrenched Jillian's heart. The current was stronger than she ever expected as she swam toward her daughter with every ounce of strength in her body. Each moment that passed, Abby seemed only a fingertip from her grasp.

When she dipped under the water, Jillian shouted, "Abby!"

Abby bobbed up again.

Finally Jillian's arms were around her daughter. With her arm around Abby's chest, Jillian managed to swim to a fallen tree near the far bank and grab hold of a branch that extended into the swiftly flowing water.

As Abby coughed up water, Jillian hung on to her, saying, "You're going to be all right. We're going to be all right."

The problem was, if she let go of the branch, she didn't know if she could get them out of the creek.

* * *

Chase was examining new buds and checking the leaves on the Aurora vines east of the winery when his mother's shout startled him. A moment later, a child's terrified cries lanced through him. Racing toward the creek, he assessed the situation in an instant. Fear gripped him as it had the night Fran had been taken to the operating room after she'd delivered their baby.

He knew the current could be swift, and he was prepared for it as he scrambled down the bank and started swimming. With long strokes, he headed for Jillian and Abby, trying to keep his mind blank to the danger posed to them, believing soon they'd both be safe in his arms and back on the bank.

When he looked up to get his bearings, he saw the fear on Jillian's face. She'd been through so much. Yet he knew she'd give her last breath to save her daughter...*his* daughter.

Even though he'd asked Jillian to marry him, he understood now that he'd kept walls around his heart. He'd kept memories of Fran padlocked inside, thinking they'd keep forever that way. But they wouldn't keep like that. He had to open his heart and let them fly free. He had to open his heart to Jillian and let her see his love. If he lost her...

The cold water began numbing his legs and arms, and he thought about his father and the years he'd lost with him. As he headed toward Jillian, he suddenly understood how easy it was for a man to screw up in a weak moment...or in a blind one.

"I'm sorry, Dad," he mouthed, not knowing if the words even left his lips. But then he felt a lightness easing the weight of the cold water dragging him down and he knew his father had heard.

Three long strokes later, he reached Jillian and Abby. Grabbing his daughter, he said, "I can't take you both at the same time. I have to get Abby out first."

He could see Jillian was cold and shivering but there was no hesitation in her voice as she said, "Just keep her safe. Please keep her safe."

He didn't want to leave Jillian there, but he had no choice. As the three-year-old wrapped her arms around his neck, he told Jillian, "I'll be back. I promise, I'll be back."

Jillian had a death grip on the tree branch and if she didn't relax, he knew she'd tire that much sooner.

He had to swim a good twenty feet until he found a place at the bank on the winery side of the creek where he could get a foothold and carry Abby out. He spotted Ralph holding on to Buff in the brush by the bank, then Chase realized Stan was hurrying toward him, towels and blankets in his arms.

Looking scared to death, his mother was holding on to Marianne, who was crying.

A moment later Chase was scrambling to the crest of the bank and lowering Abby to the ground beside them. She was shivering, but breathing normally as his mother swathed her in a blanket. She'd only been in the water a few minutes, though it had seemed like centuries. "Call 911. I have to go back for Jillian."

"Stan already called," Eleanor shouted to him as, without wasting another moment, Chase clambered down the bank into the water again. Adrenaline pumped through him as his long powerful strokes fought against the current. Then he was there at the tree, and thankfully Jillian was still hanging on for dear life.

Her lips were blue and her teeth were chattering. "You won't be able to swim back with me."

Staying calm, he assured her, "Oh, yes, I will. I'll carry you on my back if I have to. Now, come on. You've got to get out of the water."

Moving closer to her, he wrapped his arm around her waist. "Come on, Jillian, you have to let go. You have to trust me."

Although still panicked, Jillian's eyes became a darker green, and she took a deep breath. "I do trust you, Chase. I do." Then she let go.

The swim back was anything but easy. Jillian could swim, but the water was cold and she'd been in it longer than he had. Somehow, though, he managed to swim them both to the muddy bank. After he dragged her out of the water, he scrambled up first, then stretched out on his stomach and reached down to her. Her hand found his, and he pulled her up until she was sitting on the ground beside him, as muddy and exhausted as he was.

Still, she barely gave herself time to catch her breath. Then she was on her feet, stumbling toward Abby and Marianne. Abby was wrapped in a blanket, and Jillian reached arms around both girls.

Chase saw Jillian's shoulders shake and he knew she couldn't hold back sobs—sobs of relief, sobs of joy, sobs of love.

"Mommy, you're crying," Marianne said, obviously worried.

After Jillian buried her face in Marianne's neck for

a moment, she anxiously studied Abby. "I'm just happy we're all safe."

Shaking open a blanket, Eleanor wrapped it around Jillian's shoulders as sirens wailed in the distance. "From what I can see, Abby's fine—just chilled, but paramedics are on the way. They need to check you over, too." Eleanor's voice was full of motherly concern and Chase could see that affected Jillian, too.

While they waited for the paramedics to arrive, Jillian turned toward him. Color was coming back into her lips now, but her teeth were still chattering. "Can we talk, Chase? I know you're angry with me—"

Before he could tell her that anger was the farthest thing from his mind, Ralph was there with a blanket for him. He shook his head. He didn't need a blanket. He needed to tell Jillian he'd been a self-righteous fool and ask her to forgive him.

"Let's wait until the paramedics check you and Abby. Then we'll talk."

The hot, stinging nettles of the shower fell onto Jillian until she was finally warm. The paramedics had examined Abby as well as Chase and her. After communication with a doctor at the E.R., transport to the hospital had seemed unnecessary. She'd made sure Abby was one hundred percent okay before she'd left her in Eleanor's care, drinking a mug of hot chocolate. Now, as Jillian toweled her hair and then her body, she tried to figure out what she could say to Chase to close the gap between them…to connect their hearts again. She'd heard his shower running before she'd stepped into hers. Maybe if she dressed quickly, she could catch him before he went downstairs.

Slipping on her robe, she hurried into her bedroom and shut the door. But when she turned—

"Chase! I didn't expect—"

He'd been standing at the window and now he faced her. "You said you wanted to talk."

Her hair was wet and she was naked under her robe. But if he wanted to talk, now was the time to convince him that they belonged together. In a black polo shirt and khaki pants, he'd never looked more deliciously sexy. His hair was still damp as if he'd toweled it quickly and left it to dry on its own.

She approached him slowly, more nervous than she could ever imagine feeling, yet sure in her love for him. "I'm sorry. I know you said the words don't mean anything, but I had to say them again. When I saw that e-mail, it took me back into the past. I guess I'd been hanging on to it to protect myself. If I didn't let a man close, then he couldn't hurt me. But I *did* let you get close and I was scared."

She stopped for a breath, then hurried on. "I never realized trust could be a conscious choice. I love you, Chase. After you left me in the vineyard, I made the conscious choice that I was going to trust you. But today, when you swam into the creek for Abby, and then told me you'd be back for me, it wasn't a choice. I just simply trusted you. I want to marry you because I love you in a way I've never loved anyone."

When he didn't answer immediately, she was afraid her doubt had destroyed anything they'd been building between them. But then he was right there in front of her, gazing down at her, and his expression wasn't cold or removed or polite anymore.

Taking her hands in his, he looked deep into her eyes. "You're a gift to me, Jillian, a gift I never expected. I never should have reacted the way I did. I never should have gotten so angry. Your past gave you every reason to doubt. I should have known you needed more time. But most of all, I should have recognized my feelings instead of denying them. If I had told you I love you, if I had made it clear that I want to marry you because I want to wake up with you every morning, watch you play with the girls, stand beside you while you plan weddings here at Willow Creek and take you to bed every night because my body yearns for yours, then you would have had reason to trust."

"Oh, Chase." The corner of her lip trembled and she was trying desperately not to cry.

Drawing her close, he wrapped his arms around her. "I love you, Jillian. Can you forgive me for denying what I felt for far too long?"

"Of course, I can. Can you forgive me—"

He didn't give her a chance to finish the question. His lips were on hers and his kiss was taking her breath away. His hunger was exciting and real and soon had her weak-kneed and hanging on to him for support.

Finally he broke the kiss.

"I don't want to wait till fall to get married. Do you?" she asked. One look into Chase's eyes and she knew he didn't want to wait, either.

"I don't want to wait till fall. *You're* the wedding planner. How soon can we do this?"

"Three weeks," she said with certainty.

"Three weeks it is."

When he kissed her again, thoughts of flowers and

veils and two little girls dressed in bouffant dresses faded. There was only Chase, and she gave herself up to him completely.

## *Epilogue*

The scent of lilacs filled the air as spirea fell heavy with white blooms and poppies waved in the breeze. Jillian and Chase's wedding was the first to be held at Willow Creek Estates Vineyard. As Jillian followed Eleanor to the arbor where her husband-to-be stood, she knew her heart couldn't be any fuller with happiness.

Kara had walked from the winery to the arbor first, her flowered, tea-length dress blowing in the slight breeze. Marianne and Abby trailed behind her with their baskets, their pink organza dresses billowing out around them as they reached for petals to toss on the ground on their way to their father. Eleanor had been as pleased as could be when Jillian had asked her to be in the wedding, and now in her rose-colored chiffon dress, she took measured steps until she reached the girls. Then she ushered them to white wooden chairs in the front row.

Scott Paxton stood beside Chase at the arbor and both men were smiling. However, when Chase's gaze met hers, when his eyes drifted over the strapless white silk gown with its flowing skirt, something entirely different shown on his face...something more than happiness. It was appreciation of her and the future they'd have together.

At that moment, Jillian had to catch her breath and blink back tears. She loved Chase so deeply, so richly, so dearly. She wanted to shout it to the world. In a way, she would be in a few moments.

When she reached the arbor, she handed her bouquet to Kara. Her best friend smiled and took it, then everyone faded away but Chase.

"You're beautiful," he whispered as he took her hand.

"So are you," she murmured. "Handsome, I mean."

When he laughed, she laughed with him and they turned toward the minister.

Chase said his vows in a strong, sure voice and every heart-filled word wrapped around Jillian, preparing her for a future with him. She repeated her promises, trusting Chase and loving him in a way she'd never trusted or loved a man. She knew he could see that and hear that as she repeated oaths that would last a lifetime.

When it came to the exchange of rings, Scott handed Chase a diamond wedding band and he slipped it onto her finger, above an oval diamond. "This isn't just a ring, Jillian," he said detouring from the words they'd practiced. "This is a circle of love. It will remind you I will love you and our girls until my dying breath. It will enfold you in love forever. I've promised to be your husband, your love, your life partner and your friend. It's a symbol of those promises, a symbol that they're as real as I am, as real as the love I want to share with you for a lifetime."

Now tears did roll down Jillian's cheeks, but they were happy tears and she knew Chase could see that. After she took his solid gold band from Kara, she slid it onto his finger. "You will be my life, Chase, and my home. This gold band represents all the love I feel for you, the pride I have for you, the respect I will always give you. Together we'll raise our girls to understand the meaning of our promises by showing them that our love is strong and true and forever."

The minister mumbled, "I think you two have just covered my part of this."

There was soft laughter from their guests, and Chase's arm went around Jillian as they faced the minister for their final blessing.

Moments later, the reverend smiled broadly at everyone gathered. "I present to you, Mr. and Mrs. Chase Remmington."

As everyone sitting on pristine white chairs under the canopy applauded, Chase kissed his new wife thoroughly. When they broke apart, they found Marianne and Abby looking up at them with smiles and questions.

Marianne asked, "Are we married?"

As Chase hunkered down with Marianne, and Jillian with Abby, he responded, "We are definitely married."

"Time for cake, Daddy?" Abby asked hopefully as Eleanor and Stan came forward to congratulate them.

Chase grinned at her. "It's time for cake. It's time for us to celebrate. It's time for us to become a real family."

When Chase stood, he caught Jillian to him for another kiss.

Afterward, Eleanor hugged her and whispered, "Stan and I might be standing here soon. We're too old to waste any time."

Before Jillian could comment, Eleanor took Abby's and Marianne's hands, and Chase guided Jillian toward the horse-drawn carriage. Ralph held the horse as they climbed in. Chase tucked Jillian's hand into the crook of his arm and then clicked to the horse as they began their journey together…a journey for a lifetime.

\* \* \* \* \*

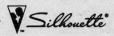

# SPECIAL EDITION™

Be there for every emotional moment
of the new miniseries

## BAYSIDE BACHELORS

and discover why readers love Judy Duarte!

*From bad boys to heroes...*
*through the love of a good woman*

She didn't believe in heroes; Hailey Conway believed in
making a good, predictable life for herself. Until San Diego
detective Nick Granger saved her from a mugger and
swept her off her feet—and into his bed. Now, with a baby
on the way and Nick haunting her dreams, Hailey knew
the rugged rebel might break her heart...or become
the hero who saved it.

# HAILEY'S HERO

## by Judy Duarte

Silhouette Special Edition #1659
On sale January 2005!

**Meet more Bayside Bachelors later this year!**
THEIR SECRET SON—Available February 2005
WORTH FIGHTING FOR—Available May 2005
THE MATCHMAKER'S DADDY—Available June 2005

*Only from Silhouette Books!*

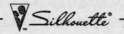